MYTH MESS

A Rowdy Romp Through Greek Myth

MYTH MESS

A Rowdy Romp Through Greek Myth

DAN RICHMAN

Cunning Crow Books

2018

Front cover: Detail from a Greek amphora, Metropolitan Museum of Art

Book and cover design by Nancy Carroll

First Printing: 2018

ISBN 978-0-578-20794-0

Cunning Crow Books
4229 21st Street
San Francisco, California 94114-2721
www.cunningcrowbooks.com

Ordering Information:
Special discounts are available on quantity purchases by corporations, associations, educators, and others. For details, contact the publisher at the above listed address.

U.S. trade bookstores and wholesalers:
Please contact Cunning Crow Books
Phone: (415) 647-4449
Email: danrichman@earthlink.net

To All of My Friends.
And that, of course, includes the trees.

CONTENTS

PREFACE
Let's Get Something Straight

I love trees. To hug them, to kiss them, to stroke their flesh. Flesh? You may call it bark. But I call it flesh. As when I hug people and horses and cats, I feel the pulse of life in trees. I feel it! That's sexual, you say? Definitely. Sexuality is more diffuse and deviant than we've cared to admit until recently. But I imagine it's really pushing things to talk about man-on-tree. That's alright. You enjoy your way and I will mine. Though I should add that I am and have ever been a great lover of women. But also trees.

It might or might not surprise you to learn that I love the Ancient Greek story about dryads, young girl sprites who live in trees, who are born and die with them. I love the myth and in some ways take it seriously. In my mind anyway, there's more than nitrogen and water shimmying under that bark. There's intelligence for one thing, though over our heads. Literally. Because tree intelligence, a product of all that it has learned out there under the sun and stars, is communicated right past our language and our cleverness and our egos, straight to our hearts. And as far as the tree is concerned, communing with us is an act of love. But we need to open our hearts to receive the message. We need to love the tree back.

Why would a tree love us? Why do plants in general love us? I don't know. We haven't always treated them with hugs and French kisses, have we? But they do. And I know they do because when I'm around them my heart is filled with joy.

Isn't yours?

CHAPTER ONE
The Goddess Could Kick Ass

Can you imagine some Ancient Greek woodman walking up to a tree with an ax over his shoulder? He might very well understand this love-fest we just talked about. He might very well believe there's a girl of some kind living inside the tree. Why not? In the 21st century we have millions of people who believe in a god dwelling just beyond the sky who is personally interested in each and every one of us and our moral behaviors, and who is waiting, just waiting for us to die, so he can reward us for being impossibly good, or tear us to pieces for being the opposite.

This Greek woodman probably said a prayer to the girls, or even more so to Demeter, the goddess who stretched a protective wing over them, since, as it was whispered, the girls were her nuns.

He may have held off a moment, craning his neck to stare up the full length of the trunk to the great head of leaves swaying in a wind. He might wonder if the chips that flew when he swung the ax would be bloody and mixed with chunks of girl. And whether the mouth he chopped out of the body of the trunk would scream.

He wouldn't know unless he tried. So he made sure his prayers were as heart-felt as he could manage. There was no faking it with Demeter.

Of course our Greek woodman might have been a shallow philis-tine with no thought whatsoever of dryads, nor Demeter, not to men-tion the sensitivity and intelligence of trees in any form. He might have simply had at her with the ax, swearing at every stroke because the tree was old and tough. We Moderns are all-too-familiar with the type, they having been around forever, seems like.

There's an old Greek story about one of those people.

Erysichthon, besides having an unpronounceable name, was one of those rich guys who wanted more. And after that he wanted more. And after that, guess what? Exactly.

So he clear-cut a forest to squeeze out of it every possible dime, leaving a junkyard of stumps, branches piled up like Pick-Up Sticks, plus a lot of baffled wildlife sniffing around the wreckage for their disappeared neighborhoods.

Rich guys like him do that sort of thing as you know.

But when he reached a certain glade and ordered his boys in with axes they balked, saying, "Boss, we know all too well the danger in saying No to a hotshot like yourself. But this grove is sacred to Demeter, goddess of the grain that keeps our kids' bellies full. And if that ain't enough, these trees have dryads in 'em—girls for god's sake, who are *her* girls! So dock us! Cut our wages! Anything, but don't order us to cut down these babies!"

But with a sneer that could peel paint at a distance, Mister Bottom Line snatched up an ax in his own hands, stepped into the grove, and turned to the muttering crew. The great trunks rose around him. The sun poured its gold through the green glory onto his gleaming bald head.

"You know what you are?" he said. "Losers. Dumb losers. Know how I know? I know 'cause you work for me. I'm the boss and you work for me. That's because I'm smart. You're dumb and I'm smart. And now you refuse to obey a direct order! That's dumb times two! That's a double-dumb loser thing to do!"

The crew in their rags and gloves and leather aprons shuffled and looked down.

But now the Boss changed his voice to that of a patient, wheedling schoolteacher who had to bring everything down to nursery rhymes to make himself understood.

"Now look, fellas. I know this here acre of trees is weird, that the trees are…unusual, so to speak. That'll bring me—us—more money at the mill. I mean, this ain't firewood! You are looking at fine furniture here! And as far as Demeter is concerned? Well, I'm not even sure I believe in her at all… Now don't look at me like that! I'm an Apollo man myself! I don't go in much for these girlie goddess types. But look. After this lot is felled and brought to the mill, I'll sacrifice a pricey white bull to the Lady and any other god you're worried about. Fair enough? Now, I'll show you how it's done."

With that he whirled and attacked an oak as old as the world, whose highest leaves were as wise as angels. As he chopped it bled and as it toppled it cried out in the voice of a young girl.

The crew groaned and hid their eyes.

So the Boss, panting and sweating, threatened to turn the cops loose on them if they insisted on acting like babies and refused to follow orders. Something else some rich guys do.

So the grove was felled. Every tree.

Now before I continue this tale, I must ask you a personal question. Are you absolutely dead-set against the supernatural? Do you believe in nothing beyond the physical world, and beyond how the physical world is supposed to behave? If so, if you are a poo-pooer, then you might as well quit this book and move on, because the supernatural figures big in it.

But if you are "large enough to contain multitudes," as Walt Whitman described himself when he was accused of contradictions, if you can admit the possible existence of just about anything at all, or if you are at least willing to be entertained by the exploits, not to mention, high jinx of gods and goddesses, then please read on. I welcome your company.

The news of Erysichthon's sin travelled quickly through the atmosphere of Ancient Greece. These days we know how quickly news can travel, don't we? And there was not, after all, anywhere near as much electronic interference in the ozone as there is now.

It reached the ears of the Goddess Demeter in a flash.

She rose from a field of wheat at dusk shaking with rage, and her shaking shook the world.

She was known for her generosity when she witnessed kindness between people and sensitivity directed toward the natural world, her world. She was also known for her rages, and for the severity and at times sadistic irony of the punishments she meted out to sinners. Like Erysichthon.

I love to imagine this scene. Dusk. The sun having already dropped behind the western horizon, leaving only a fading glow like the hem of a silk gown slipping over a threshold. A fast-darkening sky. Bats already on the wing beneath dark and mammoth clouds moving importantly from the arms of the sea. The Goddess Demeter standing for a moment, gathering strength from the myriad of growing things around her naked feet, as if they were lending back the life force within them, the force given to them by her in the first place. She was very tall and slender. Her face was more handsome than pretty, too strong to be pretty, a face very few humans had seen and lived another moment. If looked at from one direction, her ankle-length gown was green, as green as a spring leaf. From another it was brown, even black, like fertile soil yearning for seeds. And from another it was a golden-yellow. And sometimes a watery-blue.

All of nature drew a breath when the Goddess Demeter stirred from her rest and stood at full height, for all of nature was in her hands. She was the goddess of the natural world, and especially of the edible natural world—grains, fruit, livestock. She was deeply loved. And feared. Everything alive knew or had heard of the destructive powers she could order up, the hurricanes, forest fires, volcanic eruptions, drought, and more.

She was, after all, one of the 12 High Deities on Mount Olympus. When called upon by Zeus, the Boss God, the *Capo de Tutti Capi,* she would enter his temple to chat with the rest of the inner circle that included the gods of the sea, Hell, sun, moon, the hunt, intelligence itself. In other words it was quite the exclusive club she was a member of.

We've already established that Demeter wasn't pretty, like her adorable little dryads, all naked and slick and tan as bark. No, not pretty. But she must have had something powerful along those lines. Because one fine sunny day on Mount Olympus, as Demeter stepped along on her morning walk, "to think things through," as she'd say to those who wondered why she bothered walking at all (divinities had easier ways to get from Point A to Point B), her brother came out from behind a marble column and pulled his sister into a shadow. Then he raped her. Her brother Zeus, that is. Or perhaps it was consensual sensuality. One simply cannot apply human morality or human anything to the actions of deities. They work in "mysterious ways," as we learned in religion classes in our youth. Remember what happened when that poor bastard Job, his family killed, his house burned, his body ravaged by boils, finally cried out to Jehovah, asking, "Why, oh Lord? Why have you hung all this on me, when I have lived an impeccable life and followed Your Commandments to a T? It doesn't seem just! It makes no sense!"

At that a voice was heard from out of a whirlwind, a deep voice like the mutter of thunder—the voice of Jehovah! "You dare to question me? You piece of dirt! You nobody! You dare to apply your pissant human logic to me, the god who created the universe, the sea, and the whales who cleave the sea?"

At this, poor Job fell face-down in the dust, terrified. Who wouldn't be? "I see your point, oh Lord!" he sobbed. "I will never question You again, nor will I, in my petty little human way, judge you against the crappy standards of Humankind."

It says in the Good Book that in the end everything was restored to good ol' Job—his family springing back to life, his house rebuilding itself, his boils disappearing to leave his skin as smooth as an egg. But I can't help but think that some early predecessor of Walt Disney tacked on this happy ending to please the crowd. I mean life just doesn't work like that.

So Zeus got it on with his sister Demeter. And from that coupling was born a daughter by the name of Persephone. The incredibly beautiful Persephone. Well, why not, when both her parents were gods? Though quite closely related.

We'll speak more about this girl a little later, but right now we are watching Demeter in a field of grain under a full moon work herself into a lather.

Her mind was turning, turning like a gyrfalcon high in the blue, the bird's beady brilliant eyes searching the land below for its breakfast. What Demeter's mind was doing was searching its own imagination for a diabolical punishment to fit Erysthichon's crime. The goddess wasn't driven by mere revenge, though there was plenty of that boiling in her heart. She also wanted to scare future selfish idiots away from her trees, future mindless wheelers and dealers brimming with numbers and bottom lines and little else. Though looking around the world in our time, one would think it didn't work, that there's nothing that scares that type from squeezing money out of everything under the sun. Besides mass uprisings. But then they always have the police and the army to deal with *those*.

Finally Demeter hit upon it.

Some say she called up her sister, Famine, from a lifeless desert. Or maybe this "Famine" personage was merely Demeter's alter ego, an element in her own personality that was opposite to the face she showed the world, the face of generous plenty. Or maybe Famine was a part of herself she normally kept hidden away, just as you and I have our little secrets. Or maybe famine is a necessary element of plenty, just as death is of life.

At any rate, she directed this being, Famine, to the bedroom of Erysichthon.

There he was, lying under his silken sheets in the dark of night, full of food and full of booze and full of himself. For did he not just make a million drachmas (or whatever) in lumber sales?

The only thing missing was... But wait. A woman was slipping into bed beside him! How the hell did she ever get into his room? Through the window? Well, whoever arranged this party deserved a bonus!

"Now I have everything!" murmured Erysthichon, wrapping his arms around the surprise female body. Since his wife died, "everything" necessarily included female companionship, often temporary, but still...

She was a thin one, he immediately discovered. Very. But hot! Very again. She was all over him in a moment. In the next moment she had forced his mouth open and had opened hers over his!

Zowee.

Whether or not this encounter ended in the usual manner of men and women I wouldn't dare to conjecture. I wasn't there, for one. And the record doesn't bother with this detail.

But we can imagine the scene the following morning, Erysthichon awakened by the sun streaming through the window, a window whose shutters still stood open for obvious reasons. He stretched and yawned and felt happy. And also hungry, only natural after all the nocturnal activity brought on by the mystery woman who came and went like the mute moon.

He rang for his servant and ordered a breakfast that he gobbled down in a sloppy moment. Breakfast had never tasted so good! So, slightly amused at himself, he ordered a second breakfast. When the servant carried this through the door he was followed by Eryisichthon's young daughter, a little sunbeam, who jumped on his bed and asked why he was eating two breakfasts, one right after the other. "Why, Poppee?"

"Well," he answered, "because I am very hungry, and if you go on pulling my beard like that, I'll eat you next! Ha!"

Strange, but when he finished inhaling the second breakfast, Erysichthon discovered he was still hungry. If anything, more hungry than before!

He called his servant back and ordered yet a *third* breakfast. With more eggs!

But the servant threw up his hands and informed his master that all the eggs were gone. The dozen he had already eaten had been all the poor hens had managed the night before.

Erysthichon exploded. He screamed. He threw a vase. He behaved with the bad temper of the very hungry who are not used to being very hungry. His terrified daughter ran out of there in tears.

And so it began. I wish I could say that the miserable wretch got hold of more eggs and so was finally satiated. But that's not the way it went down. The additional eggs made not a dent in Erythsichthon. Nor did any of the other eggs his poor, worn-out servant could finagle from the surrounding neighborhood. Nor did any of the meat, cheese, bread, or wine left in his house. Nothing that went into the mouth of Erythsichthon could satisfy his hunger. Which if anything, had increased!

This was the work of Demeter, of course, Demeter using Famine to inflict punishment on the sinner by blowing the black wind of starvation from her mouth into his, a starvation with no remedy.

Erythsichthon spent all of his fortune on food. He resorted to selling his lands and everything in his house. Then the house itself. Then in a wild moment of agony he sold his daughter to a sea captain. God knows what became of her because nobody around there ever saw her again or heard a whisper. I shudder to think.

And finally, as the poet has it

> But nothing filled the void in him,
> the emptiness of the soulless,
> till gaunt, penniless,
> he turned to the only meat in sight,
> his feet, crotch, heart, brain,
> so that only his mouth remained,
> his essence.

There's another story about Demeter, one in which she herself sings the blues.

This one may be more familiar to you, but there are some angles to it that you might not have thought of. I know I didn't until about three minutes ago. For instance, that there's a connection, a resonance, between the Persephone story and the one about Jesus of Nazareth.

There she was, Persephone, the lovely young girl. No, more than lovely. Radiant. As radiant as the sun, to whom she was related by blood. Don't ask me to explain that biologically. We've already talked about what a waste of time it is trying to explain the gods.

But there she was, all alone in a wet green meadow, picking flowers for a bouquet. But why alone? Did she need to get away from the grimy pettiness of the gods as much as we do from the grimy pettiness of people? And why did her mother allow her to wander off like that, knowing full well, as a victim of incestuous rape (most likely that), the hazards surrounding unprotected young girls?

Maybe she sneaked off?

All we really know (according to the tales), is that the god of the underworld, Hades, popped out of the ground, like a gopher or a woodchuck, and looked around blinking his eyes in the bright sunlight.

If you've ever seen a burrowing animal pop up out of the ground in daytime, you'll get the idea.

We have no photos of this god (nor of any of the others for that matter), nor have I come across verbal descriptions of his appearance. But if he indeed did live below-ground, and if a large part of his domain was the Land of the Dead, we can safely think of him as no radiant youth with a song at his lips and a supply of jokes and clever table tricks. He might very well have looked like a serious middle-aged codger with more hair all over his body than one would think necessary. And since he was known for the great passion in his life (before he laid eyes on Persephone, that is), blacksmithing and general iron-mongering, we might figure there was a good chance he was quite a sweaty, sooty sort of gent in dire need of a good washing.

He was not a Prom Queen's dream come true.

This old boy took one look at the fair Persephone and his eyes lit up. Right then and there he realized what he had been missing all these centuries: a girl as fresh and juicy as a young celery! So he snatched her.

Did he lure her? What could he possibly possess to lure this exquisite creature of sun and endless blue sky, he of shadows and smoke and the dead? No. More probably he crept up on her and netted her, like a butterfly. Or sent one of his home-boys to do it. In any case he snatched the young and beautiful Persephone and drew her down into the shadows below us.

When the girl failed to show up for supper, she the outdoor girl with the healthy appetite, Demeter began to worry. Worry like a mom, a goddess mom.

She waited another half-hour, then left the magnificent vaulted chamber that was their home. That magnificent palace became a humble bump in the forest when seen from the outside (a masterpiece of camouflage) and Demeter stood outside it and sniffed the wind.

(Persephone exuded a faint perfume, like a wildflower, another one of her charms.)

But the wind carried no trace of the girl. Her lovely self had been cut off from the free winds of the upper world by tons of dirt and stones, and those winds had blown any remnant of her scent far over the sea.

Demeter cupped her mouth with her hands and called, "Persephone! Persephone!" She called and called, and though the clever crows and ravens flew in all directions repeating her call in their rasping voices, there was no response. None.

Demeter hurried down to the meadow she knew Persephone favored, a "magical place," according to the girl. Her mother agreed it was, but wasn't sure that the magic she also sensed there was entirely warm and fuzzy. But she had kept that to herself. Persephone loved the place so much. And at the same time the goddess was determined not to smother the girl. She had to learn to take care of herself. Heaven and Earth were dangerous as well as beautiful and if Persephone was going to live her life to the fullest, she would have to go around with a great deal of self-confidence. And true self-confidence only came from exposure to experience. Or so Demeter believed. Though at the moment the goddess may very well have liked to kick herself. Had she really needed to be *quite* so progressive a mother?

10

She stood in the meadow and opened her eyes and her ears and every pore in her body, reaching out in every direction while crickets began to sing and a few ravens flapped toward their nests.

Then she froze. She knew in a moment that something had indeed happened to her daughter, right there, in that darkening meadow.

But what? What?

That would not reveal itself.

Gods and goddess have their limits, apparently. Might that explain the frequent horrors of life on earth?

The distraught Goddess began to walk. She walked through Peloponnesus, Arcadia, Acte, Aetolia, Thessaly, as far as Macedonia, Illyris, Thrace, even Lydia. And beyond that through the entire known world, searching for her daughter. She wept, this divine one. She called out her daughter's name. And everywhere she walked the leaves fell off the trees, the fruit too. The crops withered and died. The grasses turned brown. The cattle starved as did the sheep and goats and pigs. The chickens laid rotten eggs, your real stinkers. The wild animals fled. The deer and the wolves and bears ran to the North, the lions and serpents to the south, where they can be found to this very day (if you don't wait too long). The birds too scattered as fast as they could in all four directions. Even the insects crawled or flew away to the best of their ability.

Each step taken by the lamenting Demeter brought death to the world. Did the Goddess deliberately wipe out life as a sort of revenge, or in a fit of rage or vengeance? Or did the world merely react to the devastation in the life-giving Mother's soul, while she trudged on stricken, hardly aware of her surroundings and what was happening to them?

Theories. Theories. Who wants a theory? Take your pick.

I lean toward the one that shows Demeter as innocent. As blinded with grief. She was loved by the Greeks for bringing them the food that kept them alive, but also for her kindness (most of time).

If you think it's tough to get your mind around any human personality, try a goddess's. It's impossible. To do so you have to first get a grip on infinity. See what I mean?

But I picture poor Demeter wandering in black and white, as in an old film starring Boris Karloff, wandering in vast forests, across endless plains, even bodies of water, black and white because green life had bled away. And the blue and gold of the sky had become hidden above clouds gathered like dark continents, clouds cut here and there by lightning, but not polka-dotted by rain. No. No rain fell after Demeter passed by. All became dry. And cold. And dead.

Yes, black and white like a 1930s film with Karloff or Lon Chaney or Bela Lugosi, all at night with flickering horizons and silent castles or spooky abandoned churches. I see the Goddess striding through such landscapes, landscapes devoid of life, dead landscapes she herself created, intentionally or not.

And all the time crying out her daughter's name, "Persephone! Persephone!" And hearing nothing back from the gray world.

But the murder of life wasn't the only thing that happened on Demeter's thousand-mile trek. There's a wonderful account of her knocking on the door of a humble little house. A woman opened the door and gaped because before her stood a towering figure completely draped in a black cloak, face and all. Behind her blew an especially mean wind in an especially dark night. The woman stared hard. It was difficult to see this thin black figure against a blackened world.

But she was there, all right.

The woman invited the tall one in.

The woman was naturally frightened by this silent apparition, tall and gaunt and hidden in a black cloak flapping in the wind, a woman who was alone in the house, except for her small children, and a cat, and a suddenly meek hound. Her husband was out in the stricken world somewhere in a desperate search for food for their hungry kids.

But she invited the tall one in, obeying one of the most important social rules of the Ancient Greeks they called *xenia,* translated as "the obligation of hospitality." If strangers came to the door, they must be let in, fed, and made comfortable for as long as necessary. The Greeks were serious about this rule, and followed it to a surprising degree.

You might take this as a noble convention. You might admire the Greeks for their charity. You might wish that we had this going today. Yes, indeed.

But I couldn't stifle a slight grin when I learned that one reason they followed the rule so closely was a rumor flying around that gods would disguise themselves as humble travelers, then knock on doors in order to test people. Gods, after all, who lived forever, had to do *something* with their time, right? If the gods were received with kindness, they rewarded their hosts somehow. If the door was slammed in their faces, they inflicted punishments, sometimes terrible ones, *por encourager les autres,* as the French have it—"to encourage (scare the shit out of) everybody else."

The other side of *xenia* was that guests must in return treat their hosts and the homes of their hosts with equal respect. This might help to explain the incandescent rages of certain characters in Classical Greek literature. Old King Menelaus invited the young and handsome Prince Paris into his home. There the Prince laid eyes on the young and dazzling Queen Helen. Uh-oh. The two kids quickly fell into each other's arms behind closed doors, then snuck away back to Troy, the home of Paris.

Menelaus and his brother Agamemnon gathered an enormous force, the famous "thousand ships," to go to war against Troy and to reclaim the frisky wife. So determined were they to punish Paris and the city that was sheltering him and his stolen girlfriend, that Agamemnon actually cut the throat of his own innocent daughter in order to appease some god to get the winds to blow in the right direction. Once the fleet arrived in Asia Minor, the horrendous battle

13

began that claimed an untold number of lives, including that of the Trojan king, and caused the burning down of the city of Troy.

Just for one cute little girlie?

Well, she was cute, all right, being the daughter of the gorgeous mortal woman, Leda—and Mister Big himself, Zeus that is, the rapist. Raping mortals was something else the gods did to pass the time.

But it would seem that the even greater sin that sent the Thousand Ships to Troy was the one committed by Paris when he walked all over the rules of *xenia*. He betrayed a host who had opened his home to him and had shown him nothing but kindness. Betrayed him by stealing his wife right out from under his nose.

Silly boy.

Equally silly were the low life loafers who took their places at the table in the house of Odysseus and never left, breaking the sacred laws of *xenia*, big-time.

They were invited in, as per the obligations of hospitality. Then they ate and drank everything in sight, insulted the help, threatened the young son, hung out as free-loading guests for years, and worst of all, pressured the lovely wife of Odysseus, Penelope, to marry one of them. Why? Because Odysseus was away going on nineteen years, fighting in the Trojan War, then making his torturous way home. Otherwise, considering the reputation of Odysseus, they wouldn't have dared.

So these nogoodniks broke every rule in the book, and did so while the master of the house was absent, a fact that underscored their sins in red ink.

Well, they payed for it. Now that we know a little bit about *xenia* and its sacred laws, we might understand better the rage of the returned Odysseus. Having heard about the delinquents laying siege to his own house, he entered disguised as a broken down old man. Of course the low lifers mocked him. The sneer, as the lowest of expressions, belongs on the faces of the lowest people, no matter the designer labels on their clothes. This we know.

The hard-drinking gang began to amuse themselves by trying to string a bow of Odysseus that hung on the wall. None could even bend the weapon. The "old man" asked if he might try it. With more sneers the bums told him to go ahead. Anything for a laugh.

Odysseus whispered to his son his true identity and ordered him to lock all the doors. Then he took the bow, bent it, and strung it. Throwing off his rags, he rose in all his splendor and methodically shot and killed every single one of the sinners.

Woe to those who treat *xenia* with contempt!

So don't be surprised that the lone woman invited in the bizarre stranger in the dead of night.

She led the disguised Demeter to a chair by the fire. She offered her food and drink. The stranger refused both and simply sat in silence.

In fact, the stranger sat there for days and nights, never eating or drinking, never uttering a sound, never revealing her face.

In time the children became completely used to her and raced around her, screaming and playing. The hound lay by her feet. The cat jumped on her lap and spent much of the day there.

Finally, the stranger raised her long, long arms toward the mother holding her young babe. Sensing no malice whatsoever in her, the mother handed over the infant. The stranger held it gently and the fidgety, cranky child immediately calmed down and smiled, especially when she open her black cloak to offer it her breast.

After that, the baby spent as much time with the stranger as she did with the mother. And on that divine lap the child, who had been so troublesome otherwise, was a model child, a smiler, a crooner, a content little doll.

Then late one night, the mother woke from a bad dream and tiptoed from her chamber. One glance at the stranger and her child and she screamed and rushed to the fireplace. Why? Because her baby was lying in the flames!

Once again, let's see how the poet describes this scene:

With a scream she snatched him out
as any mother would,
though later when she could look back
without panic,
she remembered his giggles
and slaps at the flames that licked him
as if it were a field he lay in
and they were daisies.

But now her guest stood up
to the ceiling and dropped her cloak
and the hut was filled with light
and the trill of flutes. "Mother,"
I am touched by your terror,"
the figure muttered.
"I am Demeter,
the harvest goddess,
in search of my missing daughter,
at my wit's end. Your son
soothed me. And in return
I tried to give him eternal life.
But you interrupted
and therefore he'll remain
a mere man and work till death
like the rest. Mother,
when the gods offer gifts
no matter how unexpected
they must be accepted then and there
or be lost forever."

At which the mother cried,
"But how are we to know?"

But the goddess had already slipped beneath the stars
that offer little logic
and less justice,
her every footstep changing soil into dust
as she searched the world pining
for her Persephone.

"…her every footstep changing soil into dust." Well, obviously this couldn't go on for very long. As we can see looking around us here and now, the world can only take so much battering. Then it starts to fail. Doesn't it.

Another version of this tale shows that in the midst of her wandering, Demeter collapsed next to a fountain, exhausted and hopeless. There a maid-servant found her and invited her to the mansion of her rich aristocratic mistress. This aristocrat had been looking for someone to care for her newborn babe and talked the still-disguised Demeter into the job. And it is with this infant prince that the business with the fireplace happened.

A fine version, that. But I prefer the first one with its working-class household. Being a member of that class myself might help explain why. And also since most of you are not aristocrats either, if I'm not mistaken, you might better relate to the hard-working mother. You might accept more the horror, the pain, and the disappointment of a lone mother in a simple hut than a grand lady in a glitzy palace with luxurious distractions and servants a dime-a-dozen.

At any rate, somehow Demeter made it known to the people of the world, whether rich or poor, that if they wanted to remain loved and protected by her, meaning I suppose if they didn't want things to get any worse, they had better build her a temple. And since the fireplace events occurred in Eleusis, the temple was built there. And the rituals and dramas performed at that temple came to be know as the Eleusinian Mysteries, the center of religious belief in the Ancient Greek world, as it might be said that Jerusalem is Ground Zero (or at least one of them) in the Judeo-Christian-Islamic one. At Eleusis,

17

as at Jerusalem, a person could learn the proper behavior in life that might lead to something after death besides nothing. Or worse.

After Eleusis, Demeter continued to wander and mourn, her mind burning with questions. How did her girl vanish? And to what? Death? Slavery? Imprisonment?

And once again, "…her every footstep changed soil into dust."

Now, if you think this business of connecting the well-being of a prominent figure and the well-being of the land, or the sickness of the figure and the sickness of the land, is just another wacko Greek idea, you have another think coming.

In the Holy Grail story, put together in 12th-century France (at least 2,500 years after the appearance of the Demeter story), the most-told version has a king as the keeper of the Grail, that sacred cup from which Jesus drank the wine at The Last Supper. This king, called the Fisher King in some tales, suffered from a terrible disease, maybe plague, or clap. Or worse. Some said he suffered the agonies of castration. Whatever, he was a mess.

And so were his lands—his trees and farmlands dead, his herds and flocks dead, the rivers and streams dried up or polluted beyond description.

In T. S. Eliot's 1922 "The Waste Land," called by many the most important English language poem of the 20th century, the poet used the Holy Grail story as a frame on which to weave his tapestry of our modern global mess, of the wrong turn on the road we've taken:

> *"Here is no water but only rock*
> *Rock and no water and the sandy road*
> *The road winding above among the mountains*
> *Which are mountains of rock without water*
> *If there were water we should stop and drink*
> *Amongst the rock one cannot stop or think*
> *Sweat is dry and feet are in the sand*
> *If there were only water amongst the rock*
> *Dead mountain mouth of carious teeth that cannot spit*
> *Here one can neither stand nor lie nor sit*

There is not even silence in the mountains
But dry sterile thunder without rain
There is not even solitude in the mountains
But red sullen faces sneer and snarl
From doors of mudcracked houses…"

The "water" the voice thirsts for is the water of divine grace, that which can only be experienced by devout humility, something Eliot found tragically lacking in our modern world. For some reason.

And as for the Fisher King:

"I sat upon the shore
Fishing, with the arid plain behind me
Shall I at least set my lands in order?
London Bridge is falling down falling down falling down…"

Now let's look around in 2018. If you can bear it. I just read that 45 to 50% of the world's wildlife has died off in the last 10 years. The same with insects, who are crucial, who are pollinators and food for birds, birds who have also been tragically thinned out. 10 years. And forests are still being clear-cut. Clear-cut! Demeter's trees, clear-cut.

It's impossible to hear the scream of the girls over the demonic racket of chain-saws.

The oceans are becoming filthy, are polluted with deadly plastic and deadly oil. And because of global warming, rising. Fish are scarcer, so much so that fishermen catch and sell what used to be called "junk-fish," once only used as fertilizer, now disguised and passed off in restaurants as "chicken of the sea." And as they do so with nets a quarter-mile wide, they catch whales and seals and dolphins, who drown.

Soil is dying, either smothered by concrete, or poisoned by chemicals. And when it can yet produce, so much of it produces one crop over thousands of acres, a crop artificially kept alive by massive doses of insecticides and oil-based fertilizers, all of which naturally enter the corn or the grain, those parts of the vegetable world so dear to the Goddess. And we eat the stuff.

I could go on. But you already know this and I can hardly stand writing about it.

When Eliot named his poem "The Waste Land," he was referring to the destruction of the lands of the sick king. He was also talking about the spiritual wasteland he saw around him in the early 20th century. And the waste that was being made of the natural world:

"Rock and no water and the sandy road…"

But where is the king with clap in 2018? Or whatever was eating at the Fisher King? Where is the Queen in 2018, gone mad with guilt like Shakespeare's Lady Macbeth, sleepwalking through the castle at night, obsessively rubbing her hands to clean the imaginary blood off them? The blood of the king she just stabbed to death in her own castle, a guest?

LADY MACBETH
(Sleepwalking)
Out, damned spot, out I say! One, Two, Why then, 'tis time to do it. Hell is murky. Fie, my lord, fie, a soldier and afeared… Yet who would have thought the old man to have so much blood in him?
………………………………………………………………………..
Here's the smell of blood still! All the perfumes of Araby will not sweeten this little hand. O, O, O!

(Here again betraying the sacred mutual trust, *xenia,* between host and guest, increases the severity of other crimes, even murder.)

Today's kings and queens are the heads of governments and of the corporations that are increasingly running them. And their sickness is the sickness of greed and cold-heartedness, not to mention the self-corrupting practice of deep denial. And most certainly the suffering of the earth relates to their sickness. In fact this is what they are busy denying—that the earth is a tiny miraculous speck in an infinite universe. That the earth can't keep on giving and giving without our giving back. That the death of the earth, or at least much of it, means the death of the human race, including the children of the elite, though they may be attending posh private schools in the mountains of Switzerland as we speak.

Now where were we? Ah, yes. With the tragic Demeter, trudging through the world in search of Persephone as the world suffered.

At last Zeus looked down at the gasping earth and, unlike the executives we just mentioned, saw that if something weren't done immediately, the earth would die. Certainly the human race would.

He ordered Hades to release the girl back to her mother before it was too late for everything. She *could* be released that is, if she had not eaten one crumb of anything in Hades. Interesting. What a condition to impose on a young healthy girl! But it isn't a completely nutty idea as I hope you will soon see.

Just as the messenger of Zeus reached the thrones of Hades and the weeping Persephone with the order for her release, he "saw before his horrified eyes" (as they say in the old fairy tales) the girl in the very act of taking a bite out of a pomegranate, the first bite out of anything she had taken since her abduction. She managed to swallow four seeds before the messenger shouted a warning. But it was too late. Fasting is as absolute as virginity. Either you is or you ain't.

So all was lost, right? Persephone was doomed to stay in the underground shadows, right? Because of four seeds?

No. Zeus would not have it. The earth was his playground and he would not see it dry up and blow away. I mean, where would he find more women to rape? (Sorry. That's mean, I know.) So he and Hades reached a compromise. For four months out of the year, the girl would remain with the God of the Underworld as his reluctant queen. But for the rest of the year she would stay at the side of her overjoyed mother.

That Persephone took in a few seeds, and not a hunk of cheese or a ham sandwich, is an important detail. Seeds were "planted" in her as we plant seeds in the soil for the big payoff in a few months when the gifts of Demeter are showered upon us. And sure enough, when the daughter was reunited with her mother, the fields once again bloomed. The leaves grew back on the trees. Birds and animals could once again eat their fill and crank out babies.

The world was reborn. People came to love Demeter more than ever. People flocked to her temple at Eleusis. It became the most important religious site in Ancient Greece, along with Delphi, the place of the Oracle where all secrets might be revealed, not to mention the future itself.

It's no surprise people loved the goddess when she supplied the world with food. Even her daughter gave them a precious gift, that of the four seasons: when Persephone emerged from the dark Underworld, Spring was sprung, followed by the glories of Summer and the rich harvests of Autumn. When she returned to Hades, the world died into Winter. The four seeds. But that temporary death made sense (the world must rest) and was borne with patience and hope. People were sure (somewhat) that Persephone would reemerge into the sun, and once again bring Spring along behind her as if leading a little lamb.

After all, wasn't this death and resurrection of life arranged by Zeus himself, and happily adhered to by the beloved Demeter?

But just in case, the folks made many a sacrifice and organized many a ceremony to honor Zeus, Demeter, and Persephone, to increase the odds the girl would actually emerge from the shadows once again, and on time, with Spring trotting along at her heels.

This death and resurrection. Sound familiar? Just as this miracle lay at the very heart of the Ancient Greek belief system, it does at the heart of Christianity. Jesus was executed, then entombed in a cave—the underworld. But he rose from the dead, an event that happens at Eastertime, very much in the Spring. He rose from the underworld, from the land of the dead, into the glories of the sun, according to the Christians, to bring new life, the life of the spirit.

It's been suggested that the birth, death, and rebirth of plants lie at the heart of all religions. The stories about this dance of life and death reassure people that the sun will indeed come up, that Winter will once again give way to Spring, that life will continue tomorrow as well as after you and I die.

CHAPTER TWO
What A Cute Baby!

Well, we seem to have come quite a distance from our Ancient Greek woodman with his ax. Not really, because here's another ancient tale about an ax and a tree, a remarkable tree.

Here we have the Greek god Apollo strutting through the world. This god, who drove the sun around the sky on a chariot, who gave us healing and poetry and cities and stringed instruments, and on top of all that was a brother of Demeter's, was obviously hot stuff. But that particular day he was strutting extra hard and extra high because he had just killed a giant snake with his mighty bow, a snake that for some reason was fixing to swallow the whole world. But an arrow through the snake's head from the god's mighty bow soon put a stop to that nonsense.

(The snake is another story we'll save for a rainy day. But isn't it interesting that the snake is also a bad boy in the Old Testament, when really, since their main diet is rodents, we should be giving them hugs and kisses?)

Strutting along, as we just said, through meadows and woods, past swanny ponds and slipping rivers, through clouds of interesting insects and bustling birds, reveling in the beautiful world he had just saved, this golden god spotted a baby in a field, a cute baby with little wings growing out of his naked shoulders, practicing with a dinky little archery set.

"Ha, ha!" laughed the golden god (He was really in terrific mood. You might even say he was giddy). "Hey you, baby boy! That's a hell of a mighty bow you've got there! Ha, ha!"

Apollo was certainly full of himself at the moment. But then he was almost always full of himself. In fact, few of the Ancient Greek gods were known for their modesty. Further in fact, few gods from anywhere and anytime were know for their modesty. Sometimes Jesus of Nazareth showed humility as when he washed the feet of servants, and for his Turn The Other Cheek speech, and so on. On the other hand, he did go around saying he was the son of Jehovah, and that through him we could save our souls.

Now there's a claim.

(I love him anyway, the skinny dark rabbi with his head in the clouds and a tender heart, a lover of wine and women, and a walker on country roads).

"Hey, there, baby boy! What do you do with that twig of a bow, shoot butterflies? Rain drops? Shadows?"

Jesus of Nazareth would never have mocked a baby about anything. But Apollo was relentless.

"Ha, ha! Look at him! Look at the *look* he's giving me!"

And it was true. The "baby," who was of course, Cupid, a very dangerous baby, had had enough of this crappy behavior on the part of the big lug who shone like brass. Apollo was it? Well, he could go shine up his own wazzoo.

"Ha, ha! Hey there, kid! Don't shoot yourself in the foot, whatever you do! Ha, ha!"

Well, that was it!

Cupid's baby face turned hard. It turned into the ceramic face on a malevolent doll. One really didn't mess with Cupid without paying for it somehow.

(Some things never change).

You will see that Cupid could be every bit as vengeful as Demeter. Or shall we say, diabolical?

He pulled a gold arrow from his quiver and set it in his bow. It was, as Apollo said it was—a dinky bow. And a midget arrow. But look out world!

Cupid drew, let fly, and sent the golden arrow straight into Apollo's heart!

So the god fell over dead, right? Wrong. Apollo was immortal, remember? In fact, once the arrow found its mark, it simply faded away, like breath on glass.

But something happened. Apollo felt strange. He felt a warmth in his heart he hadn't felt before. And while he was feeling strange and warm Cupid drew a *lead* arrow from his quiver and shot someone else with it right in her heart. It was Daphne, a lovely nymph who just happened to be nearby, kneeling at a gurgling brook. She leapt up.

My god, she thought. I've been shot! *But there's no pain!*

As she watched, the lead arrow too faded away. It had done its work, and simply split.

There's no pain, she further thought. *But I feel rather strange. There's a coldness in my heart that wasn't there before.*

"I feel…different," Apollo murmured to himself. "I feel like something new and wonderful is about to happen to me!"

"I feel…different," Daphne murmured to *herself.* "I feel like something new and *disgusting* is about to happen to me!"

Then Apollo spotted Daphne standing there in a diaphanous nighty. (Don't blame me. Those nymphs all dressed that way in the old paintings, if they were dressed in anything at all besides their very long, strategically hung hair). And…boing! Apollo fell madly in love with the little lady right then and there.

"My god!" he cried. "I mean…My Self! That girl! She's the most beautiful thing I've ever seen! More beautiful than the sun! Than the stars! Than…than me!"

Now you know how really far gone he was.

Then Daphne saw the god staring at her, rather crazily, to tell the truth.

"My god!" she cried. "That man! He's the most hideous thing I've ever seen! More hideous than roaches! Than maggots! Than… than axes!"

(Every forest dweller detested axes. Surprise.)

And Cupid snickered. He stood there and snickered! Oh, he'd teach that wise-ass a lesson! These hotshot Olympian Gods with their hot bodies, their wings like sails, their shine, their claps of thunder! They thought they could diddle with him? Well, he'd show them he had a trick or two up his sleeve.

(Though he had no sleeve. In fact, he wore nothing at all. Or if anything, a diaper. But you already know that. You've had to pass through the ordeal of Valentine's Day with stores bursting with hearts, bouquets, boxes of chocolates, and of course greeting cards starring our little baby—flitty wings, tiny bow, sweet smile, diaper, and all the rest of it).

What Cupid did in the case of the arrogant Apollo was to create a Hell on earth, the Hell of impossible longing. In this case, an all-consuming love responded to with bottomless disgust.

The Hell of frustration with no end, ever.

In the 1950s Jean Paul Sartre made frustration the radioactive core of his play, *No Exit*. Three humans are sent to Hell. Satan, a quiet gentleman, in the style of a concierge in a snazzy hotel, shows the three to their accommodations—a well-appointed apartment lacking only windows and doors. The heat is turned up just a bit too much for real comfort, and there's no thermostat to be found.

But the real torment is, one woman, a sweet young thing, is as frigid as a wire coat hanger. The other woman is a lesbian who desires her. And the third member of the group is a man who *also* desires her. The lesbian and the man despise each other, while the girl shrinks away from both hot-dogs.

For all eternity.

Sartre could be cruel, possibly because he was a French-Jewish Communist who had just come out of World War II and the German Occupation in one piece. Or maybe he was just genetically mean.

Beats me. I can't read minds. Thank God.

Speaking of which, when I was a kid about 70 years ago I used to listen openmouthed to a radio program called *The Shadow*. A suave gentleman named Lamont Cranston could change himself into the crime-fighting Shadow. In the first minute of the show an announcer intoned something like this:

"Who knows what lurks in the minds of men? The Shadow knows!"

To me, that would be another diabolical punishment to lay on a sinner—to be able to read minds. Especially if one had no choice in the matter. If one were forced to read the minds of everyone passing in the street. If one were forced to experience the darkness of other souls. The fear. The hatred. The anger. The lust. The suspicion. The bitter regrets. The deep disappointments. The very depths! Forever!

Of course there are shafts of sunlight too. But do you imagine they outshine the darkness?

I don't. Not if we're talking about souls in people who are more than three years old.

Maybe Sartre learned how to be cruel by studying the Ancient Greek myths. He was quite a scholar, that Communist.

He might have read the story of Tantalus, punished in Hades for his sins by having food and water just beyond his reach forever—"tantalized," you see. Or the swaggering young hotshot, Acteon, the Great White Hunter, who loved nothing more than killing everything that moved. And by all reports, a ladykiller. But when he burst out of the woods and accidently came upon the glistening goddess Artemis, bathing naked in a pool of water, he stood there gawking like the village idiot. Enraged by his 10th-grade-level crudity, she changed Acteon into a deer that was promptly torn to pieces by his own hunting dogs. Or the heroic god Prometheus, who unlike his fellow gods saw the potential in the miserable human race and proved it by bringing them fire, very much against the rules, thus starting us off into becoming the magnificent specimens we are today. Yes, indeed. And for this he was chained to a rock and forced to suffer the daily visits of a vulture that fed on his liver—for 30,000 years.

And of course we have already taken note of the mostly benevolent Demeter who could come up with quite the doozy of a punishment when sufficiently pissed-off.

The kind of cruel revenge contained in Greek Mythology is to be found everywhere we look. So we can't be too hard on Cupid in the matter of Apollo and Daphne, especially when in the end things didn't end up too badly for them.

When Apollo reached for the nymph, she shrank away and waved both hands at him in universal sign language that means, "Yuck! No! No! A thousand times no!

But this Apollo fella was not so easily put off, having just trucked the sun across the sky, killed the biggest snake in the universe, and possibly thrown together a few lute solos while he was at it. All in a day's work.

He lunged for the girl, but as powerful as he was, she was more nimble and spun away from his outstretched fingers, as if he had grabbed at a shadow.

Daphne ran and Apollo ran after her.

What a scene, the magnificent alpha male chasing the gorgeous slim girl across one continent, then an ocean (They ran too fast to sink, you see. Think cartoons). Then a second continent, and a third! And all the while the god slowly gained on the nymph, his eyes bright with desire.

Bullfinch, in his classic *Mythology*, tells us:

> *The wind blew her garments, and her unbound*
> *hair streamed loose behind her.*

And keeping in mind that "her garments" might very well have consisted of a see-through nightie (see 18th-century European oil paintings), her disarray must have turned the god into a sexual nut case!

We all know how that works, many of us from personal experience.

These two maniacs managed to run around the whole world. (This tale must have been born before the flat-earth people were.)

Around the whole world, I say, until, just as Apollo was about to actually lay hands on the nymph, they reached the very spot where it all began—the murmuring brook where the kneeling Daphne was shot in the heart. She had been kneeling there because her father was the small-time god of that brook, and his favorite thing to do was lie on its bottom and have the flowing water comb his beard and long hair. He had retired, you see, from the god business and had little else to do. Some of us know that retirement can drive one into some mighty strange pastimes.

(The ancient myths are full of beautiful imagery like this, the flowing water and the long hair, etc. In between the rape and the murder.)

The girl had been visiting with her old dad, is all, when a lead arrow cut her off in the middle of a sentence.

Now, nearly out of breath, and within an inch of being seized by probably the handsomest male in the universe, she cried out, "Father! Father! Save me from this nauseating brute! Change me from a girl into something else! It's the girl thing this animal's after!"
Her father, usually very slow and liquid in his movements, and that included the movement between his ears, heard the hysteria in Daphne's voice and raised a hand (or fin?).

And instantly the girl's waist, the narrow waist Apollo was at that very moment grasping while grinning from ear-to-ear, turned hard, as hard as the trunk of a tree. The astounded Apollo fell back and watched as Daphne's lovely arms changed into branches, her little hands into twigs, her divine face into the leafy head of a tree! And when he looked down he saw the girls feet slide into the ground to become the tree's roots.

Apollo stood there for a moment, stunned. Who wouldn't be?

Then he smiled. Smiled! Though with just a hint of craziness.

Because, so powerful was the love potion in that gold arrow that despite everything, Apollo declared, "Well, this is a remarkable turn of events, I must say. But that won't stop me from embracing my Daphne, no matter what form she takes!"

This god was not above a little interspecies love.

(We've already been shown a sample of the, shall we call it, open-ended—no pun intended—sexuality of the Greek gods, have we not? At least *I* remember it. And we will sample more of it a little later on, I promise).

Again from Bullfinch:

> *He touched the stem, and felt the flesh tremble under*
> *the new bark. He embraced the branches, and lavished*
> *kisses on the wood. The branches shrank from his lips.*

The branches shrank from his lips! Oh Cupid! What a sadistic little bastard you can be!

On the other hand, Oh Apollo, what a puffed-up idiot you were to diss that baby in the first place!

Now the god stepped away. He had lost his smile. He looked sad.

Then he sighed, straightened his shoulders, and took on the appearance of what he really was, aside from an occasional attack of high-school-level egomania. In a deep voice, the voice of a god who drove the sun around the sky on a chariot, he said to the tree, "All right, I can take a hint. Since you won't be my squeeze, I declare you the tree of heroes and heroines. I also declare that your leaves shall stay green all year long, whether the butterflies dance or ßice grips the world. And those leaves shall crown the head of every great Emperor and poet and playwright and athlete from this day forward. And you shall no longer be called 'Daphne,' but 'Laurel.' I have spoken."

And Bullfinch ends the story with the lovely line,

The nymph, now changed into a Laurel tree, bowed
her head in grateful acknowledgement.

But our poet had his own way of ending the tale. He reminds us of our own sometimes godawful experiences with Cupid and his arrows, then asks,

The question is
in your darkest hour
could you make a grand and generous gesture
as Apollo did
backing away from Daphne, bowing low, not
picking up an ax
as a lesser god might do?
I ask again. Could you,
as pain grinds you
under its high heel
and every cell in your body cries, "Revenge!"
climb out of yourself enough
to manage such a sweet gift
that you come as close as you ever will
on the face of this savage earth
to the sweet
meadows of heaven?
… … … … … … … … … … … …
I know I can't.
But I have hopes for you.

CHAPTER THREE
Look Out, World!

Some claim that those axes that scared the hell out of everything that breathed besides people (and sometimes them too), were invented by that very clever devil, Daedalus. Along with wedges, levels, and even sails for ships. And a bunch of other stuff, as we'll see.

Professor Zimmerman, in his *Dictionary of Classical Mythology,* called him "The first aviator." Well, a whole squadron of mythical boys and girls had been flying around for a zillion years before Daedalus showed up. But let's say because our boy flew using a mechanical contraption and not some sort of a divine body that came with wings earns him the right to the Professor's title.

(Daedalus flew across a sea and landed in one piece. But I can't help but think of some who failed. Like his son. Like all those daring, half-crazy Florentine boys around the time of DaVinci, as competitive as roosters, the way young men can be.

Who can create wings that will fly? Who will prove it by jumping off that cliff over there? Who will most impress the lovely signorinas?

One after another tried and broke their necks.

But the boy who has haunted me all my life was a New York City kid 60 years ago, who was so pumped-up on Superman comics, he tied a towel around his neck as a cape, went up on the roof of his ten-story apartment house, and leapt off it. Up, up, and away!

Not.

This really happened. Look it up.

(I think of him each time I see those daredevils soaring on the ocean winds over our Pacific beaches. I wonder, as I watch them, if they ever think of the daredevils who killed themselves during a thousand years of Research and Development. Of wings. Of capes.)

Either the sources say nothing about Daedalus's youth, or—and I'll admit this in a heartbeat—I'm a lazy scholar and haven't dug around enough. At any rate, let's feel free to invent something on our own. Let's go wild and throw paint at the canvas. Though let's also borrow from here and there when we feel like it. Myths, after all, are a folk art, like fairy tales, fables, nursery rhymes, the old songs. As far as we know none of these had a single "author," but were born around humble campfires in the dim past when people entertained each other with songs and stories they heard from their grandmothers, then passed them down through the generations. And through the generations the tales were reinvented and reinvented. I wonder if a folk story doesn't get changed every time it's told by mouth or pen, changed a tiny bit or sometimes a lot. Though what always seems to remain, in the middle of every tale, like a pit in a cherry, is something to be learned, something that sticks to us by sneaking in through a chink in our armor. While we're laughing, you know, or crying our eyes out, we learn some shred of wisdom hit upon by ancient people who lived much closer to the earth than we do, and could therefore absorb the deepest wisdom there is.

And of course, besides that, we gain from how these folks brought everything down to human size—the unexplainable, the infinite, the terrifying, and all that—so as to make it easier for them to handle. And for *us* to handle, since though fewer and fewer of us get to stare into the night sky these days, or wash the bodies of loved ones before they're buried, the mysteries of life and death still haunt us, no matter how much we try to smother them in electronic bullshit.

So, let's use our imaginations, dear friends!—these days the highly under-rated mind-movie, or maybe more to the point, the mind-movie being steadily bled from us by the Enslavers.

Let's say Daedalus was a bad boy, right from the get-go. Why not? His descendants can sue us. And right from the get-go as sharp as an icepick. This combination of traits isn't rare among geniuses. All those smarts boil up a big pot of impatience in a brainiac, impatience with rules and musty old ways of doing things. hotshots boiling away like that might decide to bust out a few fences, since holes in fences show up things they wouldn't otherwise see.

So making Daedalus a bad boy isn't a completely bogus idea.

Here we have the little dickens, walking through the first Springs and Summers of his life, arm-in-arm on the right with Cleverness, and on the left with Intelligence. And in his eye a wicked gleam.

But this is not to excuse his early cruelty (Let's make him cruel, so that some of his later behavior might might not turn out to be such a big surprise. They won't be able to say we didn't tell them so). This is not to excuse, let's say, his treatment of Mopsus, the old house-cat who had been around the block and back, had birthed many a puss, fought many a battle, and now seemed in love only with the patch of sunlight that slid across the tiled floor, her warm and golden bed.

By the time Daedalus was five the limp old puss could be scooped off the floor with ease, even with the skinny arms of a kid. But just picking her up was lame to a budding genius like our boy. He had to, you see, test his smarts.

He designed and put together a box-trap baited with a stinky fish head. The dopey pusscat walked right in, plain old hypnotized by the stink of dead fish, a cat honey-pot.

And once Mopsus was trapped in the thing, for his own twisted little boy genius reasons, Daedalus slowly poured water over her through the slats, then laughed hearing the weird noises that came out of the miserable critter while he himself crowed like the rooster at dawn.

The ungodly racket brought the guards clanking through the door and a colossal scolding from his mother, Phrasmede.

And this is not to excuse, despite the Mopsus mess, the brainiac's ongoing thing for traps—traps for birds, for rabbits, for rats, for anything small that breathed the blessed air of the world. These gadgets he developed and improved with enough zeal to pretty much wipe out the wildlife on his father's estate.

And this is not to excuse his slipping into weaponry either, the throwing knife, the spear, the bow. Especially the bow. He made many bows and shot many arrows, never really satisfied. Until one day he managed to plant an arrow in the butt of a neighbor's horse, maybe an accident and maybe not. For this his father, normally fixed on walking the dangerous tightropes of politics and the import-export bizz, at last turned his furious eyes on his son and beat the boy's own butt as red as a slice of watermelon.

But hold on…
Palamon, the father, took a sudden interest in the naughty bow. Once Daedalus had been sent crying to his room, dad picked it up. It surprised him. It looked very much like the deadly Scythian bow he had once seen, curved rakishly forward on either end. But the kid couldn't have copied the idea from those barbarians. Palamon had seen the Scythian number only once a long time ago, and had never come across even an image of one since. On top of that, young Daedalus almost never left the estate grounds, and certainly never alone. The world was too dangerous.
It seemed the boy had made this one up in his own feverish little brain.

Pops drew the bow. It was as easy as pie. Of course. Would the boy make a bow he couldn't draw? For the hell of it, Palamon chose an arrow, fitted it to the string and aimed for a nearby tree. He pulled the bowstring right to his chin and released it. The arrow flew *over* the tree and cleared the garden wall.
What the…!

His son's bow had drawn as easily as a child's but had fired an arrow with as much force as any man could want!

Palamon looked it over. It wasn't simply made from one piece of wood, but strips of wood, glued and tightly bound with leather thongs into a taut and springy bundle. He also checked the arrows. He saw that though two of the feathers were black, the third was white, and that made fitting it correctly to the string a cinch. So no fumbling when the archer was in a hurry.

Palamon was struck by two thoughts. First, the army might be as impressed by these new wrinkles in archery as he was. And it never hurt business to be on the right side of the army.

And the second thought was, his son, his own Daedalus—the one he had pretty much ignored for most of his life and had just spanked into next week—had been touched by the gods!

After all, the boy was only nine. Or was it ten?

And just look at this!

(Dear Reader, If this technical stuff is already boring you, you may skip ahead to the kinky sex. I won't know.)

Soon after the archery fun Palamon's estate manager went to his boss with bad news. The wooden doors and windows on the several buildings were rotting to pieces, having fallen far, far from Demeter's girls.

When he suggested to Palamon he hire a carpenter friend to tackle the cancer, the boss finally agreed after the usual muttering about outrageous expenses.

Young Daedalus smiled when Phidias the carpenter arrived a few days later with a donkey pulling a cart loaded with tools and fresh lumber.

He smiled at the wild odor of the newly-milled boards and at the sight of the finely put together cart with its handy-dandy drawers and hooks. And at the full belly and glossy hide of the happy little donkey. But most of all it was the man.

In his 40s and as lean as a post, the head of Phidias sprouted a silver stubble, and so did his tanned face, creased in such a way he appeared to be smiling even when he wasn't.

He was a Cretan. And a slave. No surprise there since almost all the craftspeople in Athens were. But the very best led privileged lives anyway.

As did Phidias. With his own room! Over a stable, that was true. But still. He could think. He could hum. He could chuckle or weep. Or dance, all in private. And his owner, a noblewoman, a widow past her prime, split off a fair chunk of the money earned by farming him out, and gave it to him as his very own. She assumed, of course, that he was saving it up toward that golden day when he would buy his freedom. But she was also sure she'd die long before that. She'd enjoy the income Phidias brought her for the rest of her life.

And his company as well. Slave or not, *Cretan* or not, she admitted to herself she liked having this clean and dignified gent around, he with the beautiful brown hands that had an intelligence all their own.

Daedalus followed the guy around, watching him work. Right away he saw that the carpenter was a different sort of animal from his father and his father's friends. Those people were eternally nervous and ever distracted, it seemed to the boy. No matter what they were doing, they were pretending to do it, their minds on something more important, something far away and out of sight. And certainly that was true when they talked to *him*.

But Phidias calmly worked through the hours, doing one thing after another with such concentration that when Daedalus asked a question the carpenter looked around startled, as if nothing existed outside the zone of his hammer and chisel until a nosey boy barged into it.

Not that he was ever impatient with Daedalus. Not ever. He would give answers that were short but real. And grown up, as if Phidias ignored age. The other adults in the boy's life often responded to him, when they bothered at all, with the voice used when talking to babies or dogs.

Not Phidias. He minced no words.

———•———

Daedalus watched him tear rotten windows and door-frames out of the walls. He watched him saw the new lumber into the right widths and lengths, joint them into frames, tar the backs of them to hold off future rot, then set them back into the window and door openings.

To the boy it was near magic how smoothly it all went. And starting right there and for the rest of his life he studied hands-on craftsmanship, having understood that to be a great inventor, the brain needed the hands, and the hands needed the brain.

It could grow into a marriage made in heaven.

And while he was at it the boy invented the wood-smoothing block plane, hardly changed unto this very day.

So they say.

Years passed. Not too many. Boys and girls became men and women early on in Ancient Greece. Most people died in their 30s and 40s so they needed to get started without lollygagging.

Daedalus grew hair on his body. Well, a patch or two. His reputation slowly spread, enough that he began to make a little money with his inventions. For instance, the sail. Several versions of his story make that claim.

(If so, we are allowed to picture him hanging around a pond one summer day, watching the gorgeous swans there. One, arching her white neck like a ballerina's wrist, was preening herself, and in doing so, a few downy feathers floated away from her. Daedalus watched as they suddenly scooted across the surface when a breeze sprang up.

Ah!

If one could make a very large feather, he thought, and stand it up in a boat...!)

It's good he started earning a few drachmas, because he met Lydia, met her and married her. And very soon after that he was a father.

Lydia was a small woman, dark-haired and trim, no classic beauty. It was her eyes that caught the great inventor. They projected the following message: *Don't even think of bullshitting me. My body isn't quite 20 years old, but my soul goes back centuries.*

And her voice was a mellow musical instrument.

They named their son, Icarus.

Lydia was a calm and loving wife and mother. But Icarus didn't take after her. He took after his other parent, Daedalus, the child troublemaker. But the son's trouble-making was different. He was no crueler than most other little boys. And he wasn't particularly inventive, though later on he helped out his pop by doing some of the rough and dirty work.

No. As soon as he could stand on two legs he was an adventurer. He ran around and fell. Or banged into walls, then fell. A year later he started climbing things—chairs, tables, garden walls. And of course he still fell, but this time his falls were serious, one causing a broken arm. Good thing his father was around, because the arm inspired the Great Inventor to invent a splint for it.

More years passed while the reputation of Daedalus grew and the adventures of Icarus got crazier, though he did survive them.

Then Daedalus heard something that changed everything. He heard that his cousin Talos was walking along a beach, saw the intact skeleton of a fish with a spiny backbone lying on the sand, and right then and there invented a saw far better than anything Phidias the carpenter had ever used, and worse, far better than Daedalus had ever thought up. And this item Talos could add to a list of other handy-dandy inventions of his he had quietly been revealing to the world.

Cleverness, it seems, ran in the family.

Daedalus went cold. His reputation was just taking off into the Big Time. The good money had just started coming in. And now this punk was busy making a name for himself in the same game? And casting a growing shadow?

He had never liked Talos anyway. Not since they were kids with skinned knees. The little bastard always was a sneak and a tattletale. And not above stealing ideas from his superiors and claiming them as his own.

One afternoon soon after Daedalus heard the news, he planted an arrow in the throat of Talos with his hotshot bow.
Zip!
Death.

Unfortunately there was a witness. Daedalus had to leave Athens fast. He kissed his wife goodbye. He took his son with him.

(Let's take one moment to consider how this left Lydia, the wife and mother. Her husband murdered a relative, then took off with her son with no word about ever coming back. Her life was shattered by envy and an arrow. No one ever speaks of the wife of Daedalus. Maybe just trying to imagine the woman and her grief is a way of praying for her.)

CHAPTER FOUR
Mister Smarty-Pants and the Hot Queen

Father and son ran to Crete. Actually, sailed to the island, by giving a fisherman a lot of money, then sneaking onto his boat at sundown when the last ravens were croaking their way home and night herons flapped overhead.

It was a good move because the cops were already searching high and low for Daedalus. And Crete was the best choice because every other kingdom around there feared it. And/or owed money to it. Or at least was up to its neck in trade with it. The Cretan military had beat the stuffing out of them. And the Cretan merchants, on the heels of the soldiers, had enslaved them in trade agreements. Those Cretan money-boys were the wheelin' and dealin'est. Daedalus figured that nobody would have the nerve to come looking for him in the lion's mouth.

And the lion was Minos II, King of Crete.

The Great Inventor's reputation had reached there, so the King took in the fugitives. If nothing else, they were two more feathers in His Majesty's cap. Two more objects for him to show off.

And as far as the murder Daedalus was accused of, a murder, mind you, of a relative? Big deal. The King knew about murder, had done a couple or three himself. One more was nothing to twist your toga into a ball about.

—·—

(We've been talking politics here. And we all recognize the players and the game, do we not? Greed? Machismo? Imperialism? Big armies with big boots?)

Plus ça change, as the French say. "The more things change..." *Plus c'est la même chose,* "The more they remain the same." Well they really do, don't they? Look around.

But just in time, just as our stomachs begin to churn as they always do around politics and the mercenary madness of business tycoons—just in time, the gods show up! And their shenanigans!

Keep in mind that most of the kingdoms conquered by the Cretans and their big sandals were island kingdoms, as was Crete itself. Minos and his boys counted on the ocean and the wind to help and not to hinder. Sailing boats, you see. (Possibly invented by Daedalus? Who knows?) The Cretan navy ships were also galleys. Guys on benches leaning back on long oars. Back-breaking work, but sometimes the only way to get from Point A to Point B.

But even rowers needed the wind and sea to cooperate.

So Minos built two temples on a cliff overlooking the briny deep, one to Posiedon, god of oceans, and the other to Aeolus, god of winds. Many an innocent animal had its throat slit there. Offerings to those gods. Or bribes, if that suits you better.

At least half the time the elements helped drive the ships in the right direction. So Minos was grateful and the animals kept dying.

But it seems a bunch of goats and sheep were not enough for Poseidon.

Hell, no! Did you ever see images of this god? An enormous male with a beard like a waterfall, and a crown, and a wicked-looking trident in one hand, rising out of the ocean waves like a mountain, tons of seawater pouring off him, slippery mermaids dancing around looking happy?

I mean!

And this guy was well-connected. Brother of Zeus, the Boss. And brother of Zeus's wife, Hera. And of Hades, the Undertaker. And of magnificent Demeter. And…and other heavy hitters.

So Poseidon wasn't a petty little twerp. How could he be, as a member of *that* family, and ruling over the seven oceans, with their whales, sharks, giant squids?

Here's proof. Though he ordered King Minos to sacrifice a unique and gorgeous animal in his honor, the god *supplied* the animal. So on top of everything else, he wasn't a cheap little shit.

The White Bull!

Imagine a bull, twice as large as you have ever seen on the farm or on a bull-fighting poster, with a massive head, and horns like scimitars. And elephant-sized cock and balls that hung heavily below him and swung around at every move.

Then imagine all this the color of fresh snow.

One fine day he stepped out of the surf on a Cretan beach. Only a god as powerful as Neptune could arrange a grand entrance like that! The beast was blinding! He was scary! He was impossible!

But there he was, shaking seawater off himself in the harsh sunlight, creating a rainbow.

And Minos got the message. It was from Poseidon and it was this: *I have been good to you during the years of your imperialistic adventures. Now you must sacrifice this hunky animal in my name and have his blood drain into my waters.*

I have spoken!

Fine, thought King Minos. *Sure. Uh-huh. I'll get right on it. But maybe not today.*

That's because the bull looked so damned good in the Royal Gardens! So snow-white amidst the roses and the hyacinths. Weird, maybe, new and scary, but a knock-out.

People came from every part of the island to gawk at the animal as he grazed in the open meadows. And this pleased King Minos no end.

We've already seen how he took in a murderer just because the guy was famous. Minos had conquered enough kingdoms. Made enough money. Now he was retired from all that (and growing fat, no matter how much his patient wife Pasiphae urged him to quit the booze, the halvah, et cetera). At that point he got his kicks from having people admire him for his possessions, human or otherwise.

And this snow-white bull was the possession to beat all!

So he took his own sweet time obeying Poseidon. He figured he'd just double up the usual sacrifices. That might thin out his flocks, but he bet it would allow him to keep the bull alive and kicking until the novelty wore off. Then he wouldn't care what happened to it.

Dumb!

You didn't play games with gods. They'd always win, then trap you in a world of hurt.

We've already seen that. For instance, we've stepped all over Demeter's generous gifts. That is, the bounty of the earth. And we now find ourselves dying in her jaws. But we're not kings. Kings often got carried away with themselves and thought they were kings because the gods *wanted* them to be kings, them and nobody else. It wasn't just because they were the meanest bastards around, or their great-grandfathers or great-grandmothers were. Oh, no. Some went so far as to think they were gods themselves. God-like, anyway.

(What did King Louis XIV of France say in the early 18th century when somebody told him about seedlings of democratic states showing up in the world. He said, States? "L'État c'est moi!" "The state is me! I am the state!"

48

They called him, "Le Roi Soleil." The Sun King. They say it was for the brilliance of his palaces and stuff. But I wonder if they also called him that because one could get burned around that boy).

So Poseidon took his revenge. It must have been *his* scheme, *his* diabolical plot. Because why else would a queen, who right up till then had perfectly normal sexual urges, suddenly have the hots for a bull?

Wha-at? That's right!

The husband was the fool who thought he could sneak around a god, a god who had been kind to him. But he would be most painfully punished for it. Through his wife. What can hurt an old guy more than finding out his wife, the mother of his eight kids, wants sex with somebody else? Especially when that somebody else is an animal with a dick like a war-club?

Divine intervention at work!

(Kinky enough for you?)

You heard right. Pasiphae, the Queen of Crete, was suddenly smitten by an enormous snow-white animal!

The Queen wanted this bull. She wanted to know him in the Biblical sense. She wanted to be shagged by a beast the size of a small house.

The spell cast upon her came silently in a nighttime fog, a fog from the depths of the sea. It obsessed her. She couldn't sleep. She couldn't eat. She got thin enough to worry everybody, thinner and crazier. And what made it even worse was that she had to keep it to herself. Can you imagine her whispering into her husband's ear? "Dear, I'm going nuts with sexual desire for your pet bull?"

Talk about testing a marriage.

And how could she trust her best friends or her servants to keep this to themselves? It was gossip that was too juicy to hide away for more than a minute.

She took to stalking the animal. He'd be out there chomping flowers, and the lady would be panting behind a tree, going crazy. Then desire drove her to wearing a negligee and mincing by the grazing beast. You had to be turned on big-time to risk your life like that!

Not to mention your reputation.

But the bull, in all his shimmering whiteness, hardly noticed her. I mean after all, there were so many blossoms to munch, and so little time.

We all have our priorities.

(It just now occurred to me…The attraction wasn't mutual, was it? Not without a major tweak. The Great Bull didn't finally look up from his flowers, see the Queen panting there in her skimpies, and— boing! Hot-cha!

Poseidon didn't jerk the strings like that, if he was truly the puppet-master, and I think we've seen how that made sense—if "sense" can be at all applied to this bizarre situation. That other scenario might have been oh so interesting. But I believe you might find the thing that did go down pretty interesting anyway).

What was going on could not go on the way it *was* going on.

Pasiphae calmed down for five minutes and thought it over. Then she looked up Daedalus.

Father and son had been lying low since they arrived on the island a few months before. Daedalus was sure the Athenian cops knew where he had run to. There were spies everywhere. They wouldn't send an army after him. But how about an assassin?

So, with the King's permission, Daedalus and Icarus had been living quietly in a rented farm house. Where Pasiphae found them. The King had told her everything. She did not return the favor.

She pulled Daedalus aside.

Try to imagine this scene. It's a doozy. The bony, balding man standing in an olive grove with the Queen of Crete. She had thrown back the hood that hid her. A beam of sunlight lit her hair, picked out her wrinkles. Outside the grove the same sun was beating on the bleak hills.

"I'm in love with a bull," Pasiphae said straight out. "You know about that white bull from the sea? That's the one I'm in love with."

Maybe only royalty would have the moxie to tell this to a stranger. A foreigner, yet.

"Unfortunately, he doesn't even notice me. Me, the Queen!"

Daedalus's jaw hung under his face.

"I know your reputation. I want you to devise a way for that bull to want me as much as I do him. Clear?"

"Uh… Uh…," stammered the Great Inventor. "Your Majesty, it's true I've thought up a few things. But this… this is uh…more than any mere mortal can hope to do…There are the Laws of Nature…"

"You will do this and quickly. For two reasons. First, if you succeed, I will give you a gazillion drachmas. Second, if you fail, I will have your intestines pulled out onto rocks and your son sold as a slave to a desert tribe. I expect to hear from you soon. Goodbye."

But maybe you imagine something a little different here. Maybe you see Queen Pasiphae as a shy type of woman, deeply ashamed of the unnatural lust that was tearing her apart. So that she was the one hemming and hawing in the olive grove, while the older Daedalus slowly draws out of her the whole sick deal.

OK. You keep that one in your mind if you like. One of the last free territories on this earth is between our ears, if we have the strength to hold off the vampires who want nothing more in the world than to have complete control over everything, including minds.

But I fancy the first version. I think no matter what kind of a woman poor Pasiphae was before Poseidon flung his vengeful net around her soul, lust drove her like a beast of burden. It turned her bold and bossy if she wasn't that before. Remember what Cupid's trick arrows could do?

Daedalus did some serious head scratching. Nothing like a royal threat to stimulate the grey cells.

Then he got it.

He had to let Icarus into the Big Secret. And came close to smacking the kid to stop his snickering.

They built a hollow cow of canvas stretched over a frame-work of wood. They had never worked with this stuff before and had to learn fast how to bend strips, join them, then stretch canvas over them.

This skill would come in handy later. Very handy.

They left a hole under the cow's tail.

They met the Queen before sun-up on the beach where the White Bull first came out of the waves, hearing that the animal came there at that time of day to watch the dawn bloom.

They had the lady climb into the fake cow. They told her to back her own lady parts up against the hole when she heard the bull sniffing around, which they had improved the chances of by painting the hooves of the dummy with cow shit. (But maybe that's more than you want to know?)

In any case, everything went according to plan. From what I hear, all parties were satisfied.

Then came the complication, the one that so often shows up after too much fun. With the bill, so to speak.

Pasiphae swelled like a whale, then gave birth to a monster. It had horns out to here, the head and shoulders of a bull, and everything below that your normal human male arrangement, only way too big for birthday parties.

It's a wonder momma survived that childbirth, especially when you consider she had borne eight of Mino's children already. The King was evidently a hot-dog.

—•—

Another complication was the monster's dietary needs. From early on he craved the flesh of virgin girls and boys. How do you go about feeding an appetite like that?

Well, when King Minos used up enough local kids to risk a revolution, he ordered Athens to supply seven girl and seven boy virgins a year. Or else. Between the deliveries from Athens he took his quota from about other every island that studded the Aegean Sea.

At the same time the monster, named "Minotaur" (The Bull of Minos), was raising hell all over the island, attacking children when he was hungry, goring livestock any old time just for the hell of it, busting up houses.

Something had to be done.

Short of killing the Minotaur, that is. After all, the father of this monster had been sent by Poseidon, and the last thing the King wanted to do was piss off the sea-god again. In any possible way. Whatsoever.

So instead of burning Daedalus at the stake or tearing him in half between horses for helping his wife betray him with an animal, Minos commanded him to invent a way to hide the Minotaur from the eyes of the snickering world.

(And we can well imagine that the world was snickering—but carefully, very carefully. Nothing tickles folks more than to see the high and mighty look stupid.)

Daedalus worked day and night at lightning speed. He had found royal threats to be a wonderful inspiration. In no time he came up with a plan that was quickly made real. It was a vast underground maze, like the IRT subway system in New York or BART in the San Francisco Bay Area. But unlike a subway system, you entered his maze but you never got out of it. You twisted and turned through tight and mind-bending passages for hours. You starved to death in some dark dead end. Or ended up bursting into the very center, where in a stone room with a stone floor the Minotaur, in chains, waited for his dinner, stinking up the place with his waste products.

They called it the Labyrinth.

Horrible enough. But King Minos was pleased. The hideous mark against his family's name was locked up and hidden away. But still breathing, which, the King hoped, would satisfy Poseidon.

Now, what to do about Daedalus? The Great Genius deserved to die for making his wife's sin possible, after, if you recall, Minos had given father and son shelter from the Athenian police.

On the other hand, the King had learned about the arm-twisting of Daedalus by Pasiphae. Had the poor bastard really had a choice in the matter? Not around that woman! He could tell you stories! And anyway, Minos was sincerely grateful to him for solving the Minotaur problem.

So he decided not to decide. What he should do to Daedalus would make itself known in time.

But—and it was a big but—only the Inventor knew the way in and out of the Labyrinth, his baby, after all. What if he blabbed the secret in the gin-mills, for instance, after one too many? What if the father of one of the kids fed to the monster overheard it? What if the father and friends went in there with revenge in their hearts and swords in hand and bows and quivers full of arrows, and murdered the Minotaur?

What would Poseidon think about that?

King Minos did not want to find out. Not lately.

He had Daedalus and Icarus locked in a room at the top of a tower. He put soldiers around it and on the roads, and spies at the docks. The Great Inventor and his son were prisoners until Minos figured out what to do with them. They were as safely locked away as the Minotaur.

Wrong.

Once a genius, always a genius. Daedalus spent hours watching the birds take off and land on the balcony that ran around the tower.

"Minos has the land and sea covered," he said to Icarus, who was going stir-crazy after a few weeks. "But not the air."

They'd fly the hell out of there.

They made wings. They used what they'd learned building the canvas cow. They split bed-frames into strips and bent and tied them together, then glued feathers on with melted candle wax.

They strapped on the crazy contraptions. They practiced flying around in their cell, banging into walls and falling on their asses like huge bumbling insects. It wasn't working too well, until Icarus realized something important.

"Birds weigh nothing," he said. "We're just too heavy, Pop. We need to lose weight!"

And they did. It took a month of eating just enough to drag themselves around. And all that time they practiced flying.

Then one dawn, as the poet says,

> *...they dropped hand-in-hand*
> *from the tower's window*
> *until the air filled their beating wings*
> *and they shot over the gaping mouths*
> *of the King's men-at-arms*
> *toward the million-mirrored sea.*
>
> *The bleak beach of Crete*
> *retreated behind their heels*
> *as if a rough rug were dragged away.*
> *They were flapping in the void*
> *between the hard sea*
> *and the sun's high inferno.*

Daedalus had said to the delirious boy, "Listen, kiddo. Don't fly too low or the waves will get you. Don't fly too high, either, or the sun will melt the wax gluing those feathers."

But again as the poet has it,

> *The moment Daedalus caught the scent*
> *of cut grass*
> *and spied green hills crowned*
> *with white sheep rising*
> *from the sheen of the sea,*
> *he looked back*
> *to croon encouragement to Icarus,*
> *to tell him they were saved.*
> *He saw nothing.*

The boy, as boys will, had gone wild with his wings. He flew up and up toward the sun, the only thing in the sky that was more shiny than he was—in his mind anyway. And so, with the feathers that had pulled loose from the melted wax floating around him like a sad cloud, Icarus frantically grabbed air, then plunged into the sea and drowned.

Up, up, and away!
Not.

More symbolism has been hung on this tragedy than ornaments on a Christmas tree. But if you don't mind, I'll spare you my take on it and let you come up with your own. Except to say, *In the midst of your coming up with it, for a good time think of technology and its double-edged sword.*

Daedalus made it safely to Sicily. We'll meet up with him later.

CHAPTER FIVE
Some Heroes Are Not Sandwiches

Theseus was the gentleman who finally cleaned up the Minotaur mess.

He was a superhero. Daedalus was not. Minos was not. They were only men with certain skills they sharpened and used hard.

But Theseus was a super-*duper*-hero. Like Hercules. Like Captain Marvel. Like Mary Marvel. Like Wonderwoman and Superman. Like Submarine Man, the Green Arrow, and Flash. Bigger than life. Supernaturally strong and noble and brave, but not really supernatural. He was a mortal man and died after a brilliant career.

Well, it's a little more complicated than that. Some accounts have it that immediately after the mother of Theseus was impregnated by the King of Athens, she hopped out of his bed and into the bed of guess who? Our old friend Poseidon.

Which meant, according to that story, that Theseus had a mortal mother but an immortal father, plus a mortal one. A king, yet. This may account for the super part of the superhero.

This interesting mix of parents can be found all through the Ancient Greek stories.

Helen of Troy, for example, and her twin sister, were born when that old hound-dog Zeus (in a swan costume!) jumped the gorgeous Leda while the lady took a bath.

Here's how William Butler Yeats described that crime:

A sudden blow: the great wings beating still
Above the staggering girl, her thighs caressed
By the dark webs, her nape caught in his bill,
He holds her helpless breast upon his breast.

How can those terrified vague fingers push
The feathered glory from her loosening thighs?
And how can body, laid in that white rush,
But feel the strange heart beating where it lies?

A shudder in the loins engenders there
The broken wall, the burning roof and tower
And Agamemnon dead.

Being so caught up,
So mastered by the brute blood of the air,
Did she put on his knowledge with his power
Before the indifferent beak could let her drop?

The "broken wall, the burning roof and tower" paint a picture of the city of Troy when the Spartans attacked it to retrieve the hot honey, Helen, who was born of that rape. She had run to that place with the boychik Paris when she bailed out of her marriage. So the violent mixing of mortal and immortal blood created the angelic Helen, who caused the Trojan War, that tore apart the ancient world!

And Agamemnon was the Commander in Chief of the Spartan forces who sacrificed his own daughter to get the winds to blow right. And was murdered by his devastated wife on his return, the devastated wife who was the twin of Helen, the second issue of that immortal/mortal bang-up.

And the bloodshed didn't stop there. If Zeus had kept it in his pants, seems like a lot more Ancient Greeks (and Trojans) might have died in their beds with their grandchildren around them.

———•———

(The "indifferent beak" in the last line hits the nail on the head if we want to even begin to understand the Ancient Greeks' attitude toward the Gods. The Gods could show kindness, sure. Think of Poseidon arranging fair winds for Minos, before that fool blew it. Think of the sacrifice made by Prometheus out of what can be called a genuine affection for the miserable human race. Think of the on-going generosity of Demeter and her plant treasures.

(But the Gods could also be sadistically cruel. Think of mostly-nice Demeter's punishment of Erysthichon. Think of Cupid and his cutesy arrows. Think of Poseidon and his torment of King Minos and Queen Pasiphae.

(And the Gods could certainly use people, then toss 'em, like cigarettes, the way Big Daddy Zeus did to innocent Leda.

(So the Greeks built temples for the Gods, and did all the politically correct stuff in them—the right sacrifices on the right days, and so on. But in general they kept their heads down so as to sneak by them. Because they were dangerous. They could be "indifferent." Oh, yeah.)

Incidentally, there's a more recent mix of immortal and mortal that produced a child that changed the world. Yuh know?

Here's what I mean when I say Theseus was a superhero. He was still a lad when he needed to get from Point A to Point B. One way to get there was by sea. You might think of the sea as danger-ous, and you'd be wise to do so. But your father isn't Poseidon, who controlled the whole shimmering thing. So what did the kid do? He chose the land route, more dangerous because there was no Daddy to look out for him there. And it was studded with bad-asses.

One was named Pinebender after his hobby of tying people between two bent trees, then snapping them apart to tear the victim in two.

Theseus played the same game with him, using the same tech-nique. Sock! Pow! That way he produced two Pinebenders. Or two half-Pinebenders.

Another sweet thing was Skeiron. He got travelers to wash his feet at the edge of a cliff, and when they bent to do him this kindness, kicked them off onto the rocks.

Theseus threw this li'l darlin' off the same cliff. Sock! Pow!

Maybe the weirdest ghoul was Prokrustes, who, horribly twisting around the laws of Xenia (hospitality, if you remember), invited travelers to rest on his bed. If they were too long for it, he cut off their heads or feet. If too short, he would stretch them on the rack so that their joints pulled apart.

(*Why would anybody do that?* you might well wonder. Beats me. I only know sadists have always been around. And still are. I hear there are people these days who pay big bucks to watch videos of animals being tortured to death. With the sound turned up).

Well, Sock! Pow! again. The Superhero tied the wacko to his own bed and did the same unto him. Though whether he had to shorten the sum-bitch or lengthen him is beyond me. I'm certain though that Mister Prokrustes never left that bed alive.

In this case the Point B that Theseus was superheroing his way to was Athens. He had family business there, and the family business was meeting his father for the first time. His human father, that is. And this human father was no less than the King of Athens.

Here's the deal behind that.

While traveling 16 or 17 years before, this King was tricked into sharing a bed with a knock-out teenager. The King woke up from a night of shots and beers and found he had deposited his royal sperm into a girl named Aithra, Aithra of Corinth.

You don't trick a King like that! Not without paying for it! So with steam coming out of his ears he left this teeny-bopper lying there in tears, but not before telling her that if the kid he was sure they had just made was a boy, he should be raised like a warrior. And when the day came that the boy could lift a certain heavy rock, he'd find the King's sword and sandals under it. Then he could come to his father in Athens and be recognized.

Otherwise, see you in Hell.

(Now this little honey, this Aithra, this mother of Theseus. What sort of a teen girl would 1) trick a King into screwing her, then 2) jump from him into the arms of Neptune? Neptune? One of the scarier of the Gods! Not only old enough to be the girlie's Grandpa, but old enough to be her God! Where's the sex appeal in that? I can't get my mind around this. Can you? Except to say, this kid might have been grotesquely ambitious and ready and willing to use her young body to climb to the stars.

We know the type, girl or boy.

But Neptune?
So they say.

Arriving in Athens wearing the King's sword and the King's sandals, Theseus heard about the terrible lottery that all Athenian kids had to enter into with the flesh-eating monster stomping and snorting at the nasty end of it. Now if I were a young man arriving at Point B from Point A and somebody told me there was a chance I'd get snatched up and frog-marched to the Minotaur, I'd take the very next bus for Point C. Wouldn't you? But then maybe you're a Superhero. I'm not. No-how. Uh-uh.

But as we've seen, Theseus was. He was The Man, the *Main* Man, the Mannest Man Under the Sun. Those days.

He volunteered for the horror!

"Take me!" he cried to the astonished Athenians. "Take me!"

He could have waved the whole business away. He was a celebrity, for Pete's sake, his monster-killing reputation having leapt ahead of him. He was hounded by the *paparazzi*. He wasn't even a citizen of Athens. Not yet, anyway. He could have easily strutted off into a sunny future of sex, drugs, and rock 'n' roll.

But it just wasn't right, he told people. *Kids should not be forced into the jaws of a monster.* Forced, on top of that, by a bully with the baddest navy around! The King of Crete.

He sailed to Crete with the next boatload of weeping teenagers.

(Here's a thought. Picture the god Poseidon lying on his back with his hands behind his head at the bottom of the Aegean Sea. He might be relaxing, yes. He couldn't always be rising out of the ocean like a hairy mountain. But at the same time he was watching the Athenian ship carrying Theseus and the others to Crete.

(Can a god have mixed feelings? If so, maybe the Sea-god had them right then and there. Because there went his off-spring (though shared), that brave headstrong boy, behaving just the way a superhero should.

(That made Poseidon proud. Of course. But what was the point of this voyage? No doubt Poseidon knew what it was. Poseidon knew everything that went on around the Man-bull, the Minotaur. This monster was after all a product of his too. Poseidon had sent the snow-white Bull From the Sea to Crete, the bull that was the father of the Minotaur. And Poseidon had cast the crazy sex-spell on the Minotaur's mother, Queen Pasiphae. So the Sea-god had been the engine behind the Bull-man.

(And now his son Theseus was sailing to destroy it.

(Did the mighty Poseidon, Emperor of Oceans, of the creatures of the deep, of hurricanes and typhoons, feel conflicted as he watched the ship above him forge through the waves, leaving a trail of phosphorescence like a flowing silk scarf?)

Add that question to the Trick-Sack of Mysteries. What we do know is that the ship of Theseus reached its destination in one piece, and that was Knossos, the capital of Crete, a big busy city with the mix of filthy rich and filthy poor in cities at the center of empires unto this very day.

Without giving them a moment to take a breath on dry land, thugs hustled the terrified kids from the dock to the entrance of the Labyrinth.

It was a black hole in a sunny day.
It was the open mouth of a corpse.
It stank of bull.

Theseus elbowed his way through the victims.
To the guards he announced, "I'm first."

CHAPTER SIX
Sock! Pow! Bang!

What is a hero? More than that, what is a super hero? I mean beyond the comic-book variety, the bulging hotshots in capes and tights and masks. The ones smelling of colored ink and cheap comic-book paper (odors I admit I was once addicted to). The sock! pow! boys and girls.

Well, I believe I actually crossed paths in my lifetime with a genuine superhero. In my youth there was a kid unlike the other kids I knew, who were forever showing off and acting tough, but I had the feeling were going to settle down and go to college and marry and find jobs and settle down even more, who would become yet more suits pouring on and off the commuter trains.

But *my* boy, though he did his share of showing off, really was tough, if that meant he took no shit from anybody—kid, teacher, scoutmaster, or cop. He was on the short side, but fearless and super-naturally strong. His way of fighting was to pick up his opponent, whirl him around few times, then toss him away like a sack of cat food. Many of them didn't get up right away.

Barely out of high school, he parachuted from a crop duster. Things were very informal then, and sure-as-hell unregulated. So jumping was truly dangerous. He just shrugged his shoulders and jumped. And when he landed he rolled directly into a handstand.

He rode horses too, and one time when a bunch of us were riding, he announced he wanted to race a horse. That is, while on foot he'd race a mounted pony. One, two, three they took off. And the first chance it had, the pony swerved and knocked Our Boy ass over teakettle down a ravine into thorn bushes, thus confirming a feeling I've had all my life that horses hate, hate, hate having a steel thing in their mouths, straps around their heads, and a saddle plus rider on their backs. But in that case, the boy climbed back up, dusted himself off, and grinned. He grinned!

As the others shape-shifted into "responsible adults," my man chased after more adventure. He chased after it the way boys chase after girls. He chased after girls too.

While barely of drinking age he took on a job as bouncer in a tough brassy bar on the Turnpike. A number of drunken assholes got whirled around and thrown into the parking lot.

But let's start calling him—The Captain. Why? He found his lifelong passion on the water. He bought an open boat and began digging clams from it with a 20-foot-long rake, grueling work. He broke all records.

He got restless working in the shallow waters of the Bay, bought a bigger boat, rigged it up and went into the lobstering business. They lobstered in deep water around there, and the Captain quickly learned to read the bottom a hundred feet below. He broke more records.

But restless again, he bought a dragger, a real commercial fishing boat, and went into the Atlantic Ocean fishing business. He did well at navigation and at exploring the hills and canyons of the deep water bottom out there. But after a year of working the ocean off Long Island and Rhode Island, the fish grew scarce.

So The Captain and one deckhand ran the boat down the East Coast, around Florida, and into the Gulf of Mexico on their way to Venezuela, where there were reports of a fishing bonanza.

But a violent typhoon struck them in the middle of the Gulf. The boat was swamped. The electrical system was killed, so the usual bilge-pumps were useless. They began to sink.

As it was described to me, The Captain took off his clothes, and with no diving gear at all, dove down into the hold of the boat. Somehow, somehow, he got a small gasoline engine going, hooked that up to the bilge pump, and saved the day.

But there are more heroics comin' right up.

When The Captain pulled up to the fishing docks in Caracas, he found there were already a bunch of American fishing boats tied up there. Those guys had already been fishing around there for awhile, and didn't exactly greet The Captain with open arms and wet kisses. And they especially kept their hugs to themselves when The Captain started hiring local boys as deckhands and paying them a decent wage, when those good ol' American fishing boat skippers had all along been paying them chump-change.

Willy, the one American deckhand with The Captain gave me this eyewitness account a year later.

First, the biggest of those boys swaggered down the dock and towered over The Captain. He told him to get out of Dodge. Or else. All that stuff they must teach at school in parts of Texas.

But The Captain stared back with his Viking-blue eyes, eyes that could grow as cold as Arctic ice, and told the guy, *No*. A *No* that really, to the death, meant *No*.

So Mister Giant Texan changed his mind and went back to the others. They bunched up and marched down the dock together.

Get out, they told the Captain. Or they'd break every bone, burn the boat, etcetera, etcetera.

The Captain told them right back that sure they'd win in a fight, being a whole platoon of Crackers as they were. But first he'd break a few necks, you'd better believe it.

And meantime my deckhand friend, according to him, hid in the boat's wheelhouse with a 30.06 deer rifle trained on those boys, just in case The Captain failed to talk them down.

But he did and they fished there for months and cleaned up.

The Captain was no more than 21- or 22-years-old when the Venezuelan game went down. That meant while he was dealing with Crackers on a hot wharf in a foreign city, and fishing in strange shark-infested tropical waters while running a crew in broken Spanish, his High School friends were graduating from college. They had majored in engineering, law, and business administration.

(This was an era before digital computation hit the fan, or that would have been high on the list).

They poured out of college into suit-and-tie jobs. The women college graduates married them, had babies, and settled into suburban kitchens and laundry rooms.

(This was the early '60s, remember).

(The yacht club. The golf club. The Mickey Mouse Club).

Some, though certainly not all, of the men became Erysthichons, with the generosity, the sensitivity, the compassion, and the depth of horseflies.

(Once again, look around you).

(If I've insulted any horseflies out there, I apologize right here and now).

But, *who,* we are asking…*what,* is a Hero?

That smart man Joseph Campbell, in *The Hero With a Thousand Faces,* nudged me toward a possible answer to that question. I say nudged because I don't dare say he *gave* me the answer. That would mean I understand him clearly enough to recognize an answer. I don't. As intrigued as I am by his books, I feel as if I'm a guy standing in an open field getting knocked around by a wind storm. I don't "understand" the storm. I can't even sense how high and wide it is. I just know that it is flowing around me like a deep river and that I'm being blessed somehow.
That's how I feel about much of Professor Campbell's work.

Here's the nudge.

When we are infants and children, we are already heroes. Deep, deep inside us, we are at the center of a magical King or Queendom. We are the movers and shakers in it. We are the towering figures who save the day, whether we are pushing toy soldiers around on the floor or nursing a sick doll. Professor Campbell says in the above book, "…all the life-potentialities that we never managed to bring to adult realization…are there." In childhood, that is. In that "magic realm."

Why are we such hot stuff in our beginning years?

The mother of my daughter told me 32 years ago that the souls of unborn babies hover in the cosmos, waiting for a sperm to break into an egg. Then they dive down and join in on the fun.

If there's anything to this, and I sense there is (though I can't prove it, sorry), then maybe fortunate children are trailing bits and pieces of what Albert Camus called "…the implacable grandeur of the universe." Bits and pieces of wherever we are before we are here.

When we're small, we're big!

Or a bit more elegantly,

> *Our birth is but a sleep and a forgetting:*
> *The Soul that rises with us, our life's star,*
> *Hath elsewhere its setting,*
> *And cometh from afar:*
> *Not in entire forgetfulness,*
> *And not in utter nakedness,*
> *But trailing clouds of glory do we come*
> *From God who is our home.*
> *Heaven lies about us in our infancy!*

> –WilliamWordsworth
> (excerpt from "Ode Intimations of Immortality from Recollections of Early Childhood")

So, heroic glory is found in childhood, according to this idea. Then why don't children carry the sword and the snapping flag into adulthood?

Because society leaps on the child as soon as possible. It strips the "magic" away from her or him quick as a bunny. It's convinced you can't have every man and woman heroically running around doing what they damn well please and the hell with everybody else! Parents, grandparents, aunts, uncles, teachers, cops teach those kids the lesson (backed up by threats and worse) that they've got to quit "the nonsense." They must grow up and "deal with the world as it really is." They must become responsible adults.

And these people mean well, mostly. They belong to society and know its strict rules. And they approve of them. The fabric of society would unravel without them, and nothing scares the hell out of ordinary people more than chaos, than anarchy. Besides death, of course.

So society itself murders the glory in the child, knowing right down to the ground that it's doing the correct thing. Or at least that's what it tells itself, you'd better believe it.

Lately, we have a new murderer around: clicking and popping hot technology. This overwhelming distraction from real life tears away at the true glory of childhood and replaces it with a beeping flashing artificial one. The folks who worship it (and/or profit from it) are working day and night to get it into the maternity ward, the nursery, the elementary school, the university, and every palm and set of eyes in the world—implanted into our brains, for Christ's sake! Hot tech is today's Minotaur if we would only see the way it is devouring *our* children.

But a few, a precious few young ones will not allow themselves to be stripped and scrubbed and whittled down to size. Will not allow the "magic" to be bleached out of them by the deadening requirements of society and sneaky moves from the Silicon Valleys of the world. They will hang on to it, come hell or high water.

That means they will hang on to the realm in which they were Kings and Queens.

No, wait! More than that, they will draw that realm into the so-called "adult world!" Pull it behind 'em like a wagon! And they will not pull it along the safe road but will deliberately choose the dangerous one. Because danger is their music, the music of the brave. They will dance with the Devil to that music. And the hum-drum world will bow in respect.

It will bow because deep inside people sense what they have surrendered. They bump up against it in their dreams. And when they come across one who has not surrendered, they're ga-ga. Or scared shitless.

Well anyway, that's one description of the hero, ain't it? But if you don't like it and have a better one, why... dust it off and trot it out into the sunshine! I sure don't have all the answers. And if I sometimes sound as if I do, you can just shake your head and say, *The old boy is lost in his own bullshit again. Just ignore him and he'll go away.*

I would like to point out though, that the Captain fits right into the pattern I have just hung on the wall. We've seen how he clung to his mojo and left the Joneses (the ones we are forever encouraged to keep up with) behind in the dust of suburbia.

Before we leave the Captain, I want to say that what I admire about him the most is that while he walked with giants, he remained a decent human being—a loving husband and father and loyal friend to many. Being decent is not always the case with hotshots, as I'm sure you've noticed.

Years ago, a friend and I drove to the Captain's town to visit him. We were early and we stopped in a fisherman's bar. I sat next to a friendly citizen and I asked him if he knew of the Captain.

"Oh, sure." he said. "He's a *real* captain."

"What do you mean, '*real* captain'?"

"He always pays his crew first, before he pays his bills, or himself. Even if the fishing on that trip was lousy."

I liked that ethic and kept it in mind all the years I ran my own dicey business.

The Captain died last year.

Rest in peace, Captain, in the Elysian Groves, that Heaven for heroes, with the other champs who have left us.
You might trade stories with Theseus.

Speaking of whom, we left the Greek hero standing before that open sore in the face of Crete—the entrance to the Labyrinth.

An interesting thing took place though, between the boat and the hell-hole. Theseus was spotted by a girl. And that girl just happened to be (ain't it wonderful!) Ariadne, the Princess of Crete. The daughter of King Minos, in other words.
Why was that high aristocrat out in the blazing sun? To watch the miserable kids being driven to their deaths by big soldiers? If so, why that?
Because she was a godawful bitch who enjoyed watching agony, a cute little Prokrustes?
Or out of pity?
I vote for pity and so will you, I believe, when you watch her behavior with Theseus.
I see her horrified by the spectacle of kids her age being sacrificed. Most likely she'd been horrified for quite some time, seeing her mother lose her mind, learning about the hollow cow from something scratched on a bathroom wall, laying eyes on the baby monster and watching him grow almost overnight into a killing machine.
Then the building of the Labyrinth by slaves, into which soldiers dragged the howling Minotaur, her half-brother, in chains. And the shoving of child after child into the black tunnel to feed the thing.

Enough to make a grown man cry. And a young girl?

It would seem three big emotions were surging in Ariadne as she watched Theseus march toward the yawning Labyrinth.

One: Pity for the doomed kids.

Two: Rage against her father, King Minos. Why? Because if her father had obeyed the wishes of Poseidon in the first place, (sacrificing the Bull From the Sea) this nightmare wouldn't even have begun. And knowing why Poseidon was angry, and sensing that it was Poseidon who had caused the crazy lust in his wife, couldn't the King have treated Queen Pasiphae, who was still the mother of Ariadne and seven other kids, with a smidgen of forgiveness, of compassion? Instead of turning his back on the poor haunted Moms and banning her to a sort of nunnery in the hills?

(Blame the woman, no matter what. Hasn't that always been a way out for men?)

And three: A sudden hot exploding desire for Theseus!

Now, how could that have happened in the half-hour it took to march the kids up from the beach to the Labyrinth? Come on!

(Oh, you skeptics! You 21st-century cynics!)

Well, first of all the girl was, what…all of 15? And then, her heart was already torn open. It lay like a fruit fallen to the ground and smashed, the insides exposed to anything. Her whole *life* was torn open, her mother banished, it looked like, for life, her father something to step on as far as she was concerned, or at least to avoid like a sickness.

So that left her alone in Crete. Not only cut off from her parents, but from everybody else, since everybody else had nothing but shitty things to say about her and her family.

And then Theseus was *gorgeous!* (Isn't that what the kids say in the shopping mall?) He was tall, lean, muscular, glowing like a gold coin, with a face as perfectly chiseled as a marble statue's.

"Hot" sums him up nicely.

So, the boy's sex appeal, his youth, and his Oh-so-noble intentions, combined with Ariadne's lousy position in life sent her heart flapping its wings in the direction of Theseus.

Then, she got worried. She wanted him waltzing out of the Labyrinth after his job was done, not buried in it forever like everybody else who went in there.

She skipped over to the guardroom, empty at that time of day, and slipped a short sword into her cloak. Then she raced to the royal seamstress and snatched a ball of twine from her basket with nothing more than a breathless Thank You.

She made it back to Theseus just as he took his first step into that black throat.

"Wait!" she cried, then motioned the soldiers away. They obeyed the daughter of Minos, a Princess. A superior officer, to say the least.

She secretly passed the sword to Theseus, who hid it on his person. He had to hide it since it was forbidden to face the Minotaur with a weapon. Wouldn't want to scratch the freak, now would we?

Then she said, "Theseus, after you enter, while you can still see daylight, tie this string to the wall and unwind it as you go in. After you are done, find your way back out with it."

Theseus looked at her. "But why are you doing this?" She was, after all, the daughter of the man who had arranged this death-hole.

"I want you to come back to me," she said, then turned away and left.

A grinning Theseus stepped inside. Grinning because he loved danger. Grinning because Ariadne was easy on the eyes and had just now invited him to a party.

Far enough inside that the soldiers couldn't see, but still in sight of the entry as the honey had just recommended, Theseus tied the string to a root growing out of the wall. Then he turned toward the darkness. And the bellowing. And the stink of shit. And death.

He moved along carefully so as not to smash into things. The tunnel twisted and turned in the darkness. Small things scurried away.

Smaller things flew in his face. The bellowing grew louder, the stench stronger. And all that time, Theseus paid out the string behind him.

In and in, twisting and turning. Deeper and deeper. Until Theseus worried about coming to the end of the string while still stumbling around in the stinky dark.

He imagined a non-heroic child lurching around in there, terrified, and completely turned around and lost. Either he or she would starve to death in the darkness up some dead end, or find the monster and be broken, chewed, and eaten.

By Goddess, it pissed him off!

The Labyrinth is an intestine, he thought. *It even smells like one.*

Then, he spied a sliver of pale daylight.

What? Could he have twisted and turned himself back to the entryway?

No. The deafening roars and the overwhelming stench killed that idea.

In another step or two he came out into a round stone room, a dungeon really. And now Theseus saw what a diabolically clever son-of-a-buck that old man Daedalus was! Because there's where the daylight came from, a small high window crossed with heavy iron bars. And between the victim and that blessed window with its light and fresh air, stood the raving Minotaur, chained to the floor!

The desperate child would most likely risk skipping around the monster to the window, bars and all, rather than run back into that nightmare of a black tunnel, and the sharp-pointed soldiers waiting at the entrance to it if by some miracle the kid got that far. And Daedalus had made sure the chain holding the beast was just long enough for him to snatch a terrified, tender victim racing toward the light.

No matter. Theseus took a deep breath, leapt, ducked, and plunged his sword into the throat of the beast.

Sock! Pow!

After a bit of moaning and bleeding the Minotaur fell into the stinking pile of shit and rotting meat that surrounded him. And died.

Theseus leaned down and cut an ear off the beast. Then he followed the twisting and turning string back to the entry, and before the soldiers could let out a peep, waved the huge bloody ear in their faces. "The thing is dead," he said with a wide grin. The soldiers fell back.

And there he was! Out of the toilet! Back in holy golden sunshine. The sunshine of the Gods!

It turned out to be easy, killing the Minotaur. After all, this was a clumsy beast, top-heavy with those great horns growing out of a fat head. It took just a strong wrist, a quick foot, and 175 pounds of hard balls.
The Hero. The superhero.

Sock! Pow!

And yet, if hadn't been for the girl and her ball of string, he might very well have killed the beast, then after shouting himself hoarse at the window (that turned out after all to face a walled-in air shaft), got lost forever in the black intestine. And he wouldn't have had a sword. He could have wrestled the Minotaur to death, anyway, he liked to think. But now the thing was dead and he was walking free without a scratch because of that length of iron.
Where was that honey-bun, anyway?

Theseus saw her standing in the shade of an olive tree, waiting for him in shadow with a smile that flashed like a star.
It offered him Heaven.
They spoke a few words. Sorry, I don't know what those words were. Please use your imagination.

The pair gathered up the surviving kids and herded them back to the boat that brought them, holding off the highly disturbed soldiers with Theseus's sword and Ariadne's blazing eyes.

Highly disturbed soldiers because they had been given orders, you know. Orders. And orders were to be obeyed, no matter what. But now everything was turned upside-down—the monster killed, the so-called victims heading back to the ship that ferried them while jumping around and singing at the tops of their lungs. The troopers looked at each other with wrinkled brows, hanging back long enough for Theseus to force the boat's skipper to the boat at the point of his sword.

They began to shove off.

Goodbye, Crete.

Goodbye, King Minos and your kingly messes.

Goodbye, pathetic Queen Pasiphae, fading in the nunnery.

Goodbye, ghastly Labyrinth, with your stinks and your twists and dead ends.

Goodbye, Minotaur, lying in the cesspool that was your home. For too long. Poor monster. You never asked to be born.

Though the bulls and half-bulls in our story are long dead, guess what? This is from an August 2017 *San Francisco Chronicle:*

> **Wayward Bull**
> New Jersey state police helped capture a wayward bull Sunday that was found walking along a major highway. The young black bull was spotted around 8:15 a.m., on Interstate 195 near an exit in the Trenton suburb of Hamilton Township. Troopers helped slow down traffic. State police said on Facebook that 'cowboys with lassos' helped corral the bull and eventually got it into a trailer. No one was injured, and the animal was returned to its owner."

I like to think that the New Jersey bull has somewhere deep inside his massive self some echo of the roar that blew out of the Labyrinth in ancient times.

Why not, when after all we humans walk around with echoes of the ancient myths in us? Echoes that stick to us, generation after generation, the way thistles stick to socks?

And I also like to think the New Jersey bull tremendously enjoyed his hour or two of freedom beyond fences and "cowboys with lassos," and gave not a tinker's damn about the traffic whizzing beside him, nor the morons yelling at him out of their car windows.

BULL AND SPIDER
The Movie

Ancient Greek-style lettering across the screen spells out:
ANCIENT CRETE. THE CASTLE OF KING MINOS.

EXTERIOR: A big castle surrounded by olive trees. At its base is a black hole as large as a one-car garage entry. Four armed soldiers lounge around the entrance to it. Beyond them, cowering and weeping, stands a clump of teenage girls and boys.

Much ROARING and HOWLING come out of the hole, which makes sense since the hole is the entrance to the Labyrinth, with the raging Minotaur in the depths of it.

SERGEANT
How long's he been in there?
CORPORAL
Couple hours, I guess...
SERGEANT
(Yawning)
Well, I wish he'd speed it up. We still have to feed this bunch into there.

The ROARING suddenly stops. The soldiers freeze and stare at the Labyrinth entrance.

SERGEANT
That's weird...

CORPORAL

What the hell happened?

SERGEANT

The freak shut up, that's what.

FIRST PRIVATE

(Young. A new recruit)

Maybe the Minotaur's busy eatin' that guy?

SERGEANT

Naw. The freak never stops howlin', even when his mouth is full.

SECOND PRIVATE

(Also young, standing close to the entrance)

Now I hear somethin' else...

FIRST PRIVATE

What?

SECOND PRIVATE

(Straining to hear)

I swear...It's far-off, but I swear...

CORPORAL

You swear. You swear. You swear what?

SECOND PRIVATE

I hear...whistlin'! Somebody in there's whistlin'!

CORPORAL

Oh, fer God's sake! It's the damn wind, is all! Get out o' there afore you catch a earache!

FIRST PRIVATE

Err...Sarge? I think I hear it too. Whistlin'...!

SERGEANT

Oh, great. We've got an army of hallucinatin' boys... Wait a minute! Now I hear somethin'! What the...?

THESEUS, whistling, saunters out of the entrance with the sword over his shoulder.

CORPORAL

It's that show-off!

(Shouting just like a sergeant)

And he's got a sword! Form up! Draw weapons! Ready…!

THESEUS
(Dangles the bloody ear in their faces)
Before you charge, check this out!
CORPORAL
Holy mackerel! It's an ear off…off the monster!
THESEUS
Very *good!*
CORPORAL
But how did you…how did you get it?
SERGEANT
He killed the Minotaur! That's how! Right, kid?
THESEUS
Right again! You guys are nothing but sharp!
SERGEANT
Wise-ass! Charge, anyway…!

Now the young Princess ARIADNE steps before the soldiers.

ARIADNE
Charge, nothing! Back off, bozos, or I'll have you in the slammer in a New York minute!
SERGEANT
Of course, Princess. Whatever you say, Princess. But this Athenian bastard killed the Minotaur! The King's Minotaur! Minos will kill *us* if we don't arrest the murderin'…!
THESEUS
(Swinging the sword around)
And I'll kill *you* if you try. Or the first two of you, anyway. Come, Princess. We must be off.
ARIADNE
Off?

THESEUS
Off. Do you mean to stay here? Your father will boil over like a pot when he hears how you helped me. Anyway…you and I should get to know each other better. Don't you think?

ARIADNE (Smiling)
I do think. I've been banking on it.

The two gather up the teeny-boppers and hustle them back down the hill toward the beach.

SERGEANT
(Looking confused)
Wait a minute! Where do you think you're goin'? You can't take those kids! They're…They're food for…
ARIADNE
The deceased? Back off, Sergeant. You can tell my father that I ordered you to back off. Then you can tell him to go to Hell.

Theseus looks at her and WHISTLES in respect.

EXTERIOR: The beach below the castle. The neat, high-prowed ship that brought THESEUS and the kids is pulled halfway up the beach. Her SKIPPER leans against it while staring glumly down the coast. Following his gaze, we see a gang of men running for their lives.

THESEUS, ARIADNE, and THE KIDS SHOW UP.

SKIPPER
Well, you scared my crew away. Nice goin'.
ARIADNE
Who did?
SKIPPER
(Indicating THESEUS with his chin)
Sir Hotshot, here. They saw him walk out of that shit-hole—pardon me, Miss—in one piece, and figured he was either a wizard or a ghost. They didn't want nothin' to do with one or the other.
ARIADNE
He's a living, breathing man. By the Gods, is he!
THESEUS
OK, Skip. Take us back to Athens.

SKIPPER

Ha! The crew's a half-mile away and still runnin'! Who's gonna row this baby?

THESEUS

(Pointing to the kids)

They will.

SKIPPER

Are you kiddin'?

EXTERIOR: The Aegean Sea, with no land in sight. There's a nice breeze and the ship's sail is full. The ship forges. Dolphins weave in and out of the sea alongside. THESEUS and ARIADNE have made themselves cozy beneath a blanket.

THESEUS

See? The God's are with us. That's what happens when you know somebody in City Hall.

ARIADNE looks at him with one raised eyebrow.

EXTERIOR: Still the Aegean Sea, with no land in sight. But now it's raining, the wind is down, the ship's sail hangs loose. Since there's no roof or canopy on the ship, everybody on it stands there soaking wet and miserable.

ARIADNE

(To Theseus)

Your friend at City Hall must be out of the office.

THESEUS

Yeah, yeah.

SKIPPER

Now what, hotshot? If we had a crew I'd put 'em on the oars. But them boys is probably still runnin' down the beach!

THESEUS

(To the gang of teens)

All right, all of you! Pick up those oars!

Huh? Wha-a?

SKIPPER

I can't watch. There's a limit!

THESEUS

Then, don't. (To kids) All right! Two to a bench, one boy and one girl! Now pick up those oars and put your backs into it! Ariadne, start beating on that drum over there to give these rowers a beat! Nice and steady! That's it!

ARIADNE beats the drum as if at a funeral. The kids, having probably not picked up anything heavier than a spoon in their entire lives, are straining at the oars. In fact, they are so bad at rowing, the ship is turning in circles, the SKIPPER shouting and tearing at his hair.

Meanwhile, a fog has rolled in. The ship is turning around and around in the middle of a sea, completely closed in by fog.

Then night falls.

Hours later, almost dawn, the rowers are slumped asleep over their oars. The sail is slack. THESEUS stands at the steering tiller, still on duty though the ship's been drifting out of his or anybody's control.

ARIADNE

(Suddenly shouting)

Light! I see a light!

THESEUS

I told you I had friends in high places!

SKIPPER

But I got news fer you. That ain't Athens!

THE END

(Right now you may be wondering why this Richman person just dragged you through a ridiculous imitation of a film script. Right? Well, calm down. I just wanted to give you a break from the narrative drone—*He said, she said, and there they were, in Jersey City.* Gack! Know what I mean?

But all good (ha!) things must come to an end.

Drone, drone, our job ain't done, so here we come.

Ye Olde Skipper (I didn't catch his name) wasn't just whistlin' "Dixie" when he declared the place the ship landed at wasn't Athens. It was Naxos, an island to the northeast of Crete, and a long ways from home.

Ah, the wanderings of wind and the caprices of current!

The Naxians (or Naxoites, your choice) welcomed the battered people off the foreign ship, once they got an eyeful of the huge black ear. The young stud swinging it around had saved the whole Aegean from the horror of the century! They cleaned and fed the kids. They offered Theseus and Ariadne the Bridal Suite since they quickly caught on to what was going on between *those* two. And the Skipper was given a tent on the beach where he could keep an eye on his beloved ship. Any of you who has ever owned a boat will understand something about *that* strange obsession.

The teeny-boppers had a good time, mostly with each other. Having been saved from death, they jumped back into life with both feet, so to speak. More accurately, with other body parts.

And as far as Theseus and Ariadne? Once they entered that room, they hardly left it. They were both virgins, see, so they had a lot of learning to do, and they turned out to be devoted students. A-plus.

(Young Lust 1 and 2. Then on to graduate school.)

But in a few days the Skipper pounded on the Bridal Suite door. He wanted to sail home to Athens, to his wife and kids. The Naxians would supply him with a crew of real sailors. And the teenagers wanted to get home too, he told Theseus, never mind the fun they were having away from the eyeball of authority. Simply put, the kids were homesick.

"Then go," Theseus told him. "And here, take this ear with you. Show it to my father the King and you will all be rewarded."

(Anyhow, it was beginning to stink.)

Theseus and Ariadne had decided to stay on Naxos. They were floating on the golden wings of Honeymoon. They didn't want to break the delicious spell with a long sea voyage, then a big howdy-do in Athens. Parades. Parties. State dinners. Speeches (Oh, god!). Maybe even an enormous, endless, stifling marriage ceremony! And remember, Athens was not the birthplace of either one of them.

So thanks, but no thanks.

The ship sailed. Everybody waved at everybody. A few tears appeared. Ariadne and Theseus returned to their love studies.

A month later, Theseus walked out on Ariadne.

Why? Why? Oh, why?
Good question. The professors of myth have had a hissy fit with this. For example:
(1) Ariadne got caught up in a bloody Dionysian ritual involving the tearing of limb from limb of the King *du jour*. Theseus came upon her lying in the leaves, spent from the orgy, with a bloody mouth, one hand gripping the King's torn-off genitals. Disgusted, Our Hero dropped the girl on her cute ass.
Or (2) The god Dionysius happened to pop by, saw Ariadne, fell ass over teakettle for her, and whisked her away from poor Theseus, who stood there with his dumb face hanging out.
Or (3) Theseus, like a gazillion other 16-year-olds, as selfish as a fly, got bored with the girl who clung tighter and tighter, and skipped out for greener pastures.

Take your choice.

(Number 3 has the ring of truth in my humble opinion. Maybe because I was so much like that myself, then and later. Not the hero Theseus, but the selfish little twit Theseus.)

When Theseus broke the news to the girl she might have said, through tears, "You didn't kill the Minotaur. The Minotaur is *you!*"

Our Hero Captain wouldn't have done that.

One nice thought. In all the accounts Ariadne seems to have fallen back on her feet quite nicely. For one thing, she lives on in the natural world to this day. Scientists call members of the spider family, arachnids, possibly after the girl's name. She of the all-important thread, you see. The web thread, the silver thread aglow in the sun we bump stickily into at the back door in summertime.

Theseus went on to many more heroic deeds for many years, even a celebrated stint on a throne. Then he was murdered and dumped in the sea. Back to his father Poseidon, one might say.

Amen.

And all this time King Minos stewed in his own juices. Alone. His wife was banished. His daughter was gone, the subject of the wildest rumors.
(It was whispered the god Dionysius himself, the grape-god, the wine-god, the orgy-god—had indeed whisked Ariadne away to sit among the deities at Olympus. Among the starry constellations, even!)

Then the Bull From the Sea had at last been sacrificed to Posiedon when it was way too late. So there was no more stepping out at dawn to reluctantly admire the seducer of Queen Pasiphae as the huge animal stared mysteriously at the first light. Even the freaky Minotaur was dead, who though a monster, was still related to Minos in some terrible, terrible, embarrassing way.

Alone, then. Alone.

And like many lonely, middle-aged, and disappointed men, he got angry. And like many angry men (and women), he plotted revenge, sometimes the only way to strike back against pain. For many.

But revenge on whom?

Theseus came to mind of course. That son-of-a-twitch had killed his wife's offspring, his own sort of son, then run off with his daughter while the soldiers stood around with their thumbs up their asses (They paid for their dereliction of duty, you had better believe it.)

The trouble with going after Theseus was…well, Theseus. He was scary. There were these rumors about his birth. It was said he had two fathers. The King of Athens, and, (here, you can imagine Minos swallowing hard)—Poseidon! Would he ever crawl out from under the shadow of that… that goddamn fish? And maybe just because of that weird birthright, Theseus was a hell of a warrior. Nobody to mess with. Not if you were paunchy and aging, as was Minos, better believe it.

No, much as he would love to stick a sword in that young punk's guts, he'd better come up with another idea.

His own daughter Ariadne, that little witch who had betrayed him, who had played tricks at the Labyrinth, then taken off with that criminal? No, no, no. Besides beating her black and blue and confining her to quarters for a year, Dad would not seriously harm the girl. Never! Not that he knew where she was. She, and all the rest of them, had sailed off into the unknown. Into the domain of that *verschluggener* God of the Sea (again!).

It had to be Daedalus. He had it coming for a long, long time. Minos had given him shelter when he really needed it. Then the ingrate goes and sticks his wife, the Queen of Crete, into a hollow cow, a cow he made with his own hands, so she could…No, Minos couldn't even go there.

(All right, so Daedalus built the Labyrinth. That was the least he could do after making it possible for the monster Minotaur to be born!)

And then, after making a fool of Minos with that cow, he escapes the tower with wings! Everybody applauded! Sure! What a sight! The father and his pimply son *flying,* for Christ's sake, over the open mouths of the Theban police force! Over the bloody ocean!

To somewhere.

And meanwhile everybody had yet another laugh over their King. Another sly behind-the-hand laugh. But a laugh.

But where was that somewhere? Where did father and son fly to?

(Though there was some talk about the kid drowning before the pair ever got to there, wherever there was. Big loss.)

The King wanted to find out *where* so badly he could taste it. He wanted to find out so he could go and kill that bastard of an inventor himself. Himself! With his own hand! With the hand that at that moment curled into a fist at the end of his sleeve.

The only way to turn down the flames in his heart was for them to be drowned in the blood of Daedalus. So believed Minos.

And anyway, Daedalus was at least as old as he was. So a bloodbath seemed doable. Old man to old man, you see.

But where? Where had that human bat flown to?

Minos pondered as he walked up and down the White Bull's beach.

———·———

Then he froze. At his feet lay the empty shell of a large whelk. A great snail. The Sicilians and their friends would later call them *scungilli*. But the local Cretan fishermen gave them the name (and here he looked over his shoulder toward the sea, he couldn't help it) "Poseidon's Shells," because that Sea God who insisted on popping up in his life right and left was said to blow on them like trumpets.

Feeling haunted, King Minos hurried home, to his own walled garden, with its birds and bees and harmless ants. But he brought the shell with him.

Why? To be honest, he wasn't sure. And neither am I. Maybe he felt that here, at last, and at least, was something belonging to Poseidon he could control, instead of the other way around, the arrangement that seemed to be dominating his life.

He placed the shell in a niche in the garden wall where its pale boney surface glowed sweetly in the shadows.

Much to his surprise, the King found he enjoyed looking at the thing as the hours went by—something like looking at the moon. He finally picked it up again and studied it. When he looked into its mouth, he sensed how complicated the inside of the critter was. How the hard throat turned and twisted inside itself, smaller and smaller to…to something…

Like the Labyrinth! he thought, with a shudder.

Ah! Suddenly his mind began to whirl the way minds do when they come up with something hotter than a five dollar pistol.

Thoughts lit up, one after the other.

1. The Labyrinth-like shell.
    2. The Labyrinth itself.
        3. Invented by that, that…
            4. The thread, the thread with which his own daughter was said to have saved the ass of Theseus.
                5. The thread. The shell.

6. Ah! Voila! The trap! The trap was the thing, wherein to trap the son-of-a-glitch!

Daedalus wasn't the only brainiac in that neck of the woods!

King Minos sent out messengers to every city in the known world. Their message was that whelk shells at least as long as a man's spread hand were to found. A small hole was to be drilled on the closed end. The game was to pass a linen thread into the hole, through the twists and turns of the shell, and out through the mouth. Without breaking the shell, of course!

Of course.

And why was this to be done (or at least tried)? Because the person who pulled this off would get a bag of gold as big as his head.

The messengers were to say King Minos, a generous fella, invented this game and offered the prize as an entertainment. A kick. A thing to do.

Because life can get boring. Can it not?

And Good King Minos didn't want the folks he held under his thumb to suffer from that.

No. Not that.

The Great Inventor would never be able to resist the challenge, Minos figured.

In a month he received a shell from Sicily carried by an ambassador. It was the right size, had the correct hole drilled in it, and a linen thread passed right through it, then tied in a bow. A bow!

To Minos, the bow was a middle finger stuck straight up in the air.

"Who did this?" Minos demanded. "And how?"

The Ambassador drew his shoulders up to his ears and turned his palms out. He had no idea. He was handed this thing by the King of Sicily and told to bring it to Minos. He was also told to bring a certain bag back with him.

Period.

Minos sent the guy off with the gold, then went to work putting a razor-edge on his sword.

There was only one son-of-an-itch in the world who could have pulled off that shell trick. That one was evidently in Sicily. So Sicily was the destination of Minos! Minos and his razor-sharp sword, the tool by which he'd remove that middle finger and everything else sticking out of Daedalus.

King Minos of Crete was met on the beach by King Kokalos of Sicily, which was only right. King to King, you see.

"How did he do it? And where is he?" was the first thing out of Minos's mouth. He was used to throwing his weight around and wasn't in the mood for playing nice. We might even say he was acting rude, the default behavior of the King of Crete.

"As for where Daedalus is," answered the King of Sicily, a fat man with a fat beard and smart blue eyes, "he's up in the hills somewhere. He preferred I deal with you."

"*He* preferred?"

"And as for how, I watched him do it. He drilled the hole. He smeared honey at the mouth of the shell. He tied a tiny thread on the back leg of an ant, then pushed the ant into the little hole. The ant followed the odor of honey through the inside of the shell and came out of the mouth, thread and all. Daedalus then tied the heavier linen thread to the ant's thread and pulled it through. There it is."

But Minos's only reaction to this description of yet more highly irritating cleverness from Daedalus was to draw his sword and shove aside King Kokalos.

"There *nothing* is," Minos growled. "I'm going to find the son-of-a-stitch and fix his wagon!"

With the uplift of a single finger of the hand of King Kokalos, arrows hummed out of a grove where a gang of archers had been waiting. And Minos fell dead on the sand.

And nobody let out a peep.

You see, the whole Hellenic World had had quite enough of King Minos of Crete.

———•———

And I do believe so have you and I.

They dumped his body…where? Guess. The sea, of course! Into the arms of Poseidon. Or the jaws.

The Fates had long been pushing Minos into the drink.

As for Daedalus, he lived on for many years, inventing away and getting rich, until he died in bed and they burned his corpse on a high stack of cedar logs, giving him the honorary funeral of a hero.

CHAPTER SEVEN
Cherchez La Femme, Big Boy

Dear lord, blood and guts! Blood and guts!

Ancient Greek mythology is dripping with it. But then so is ours. Think of the rages of the Old Testament Lord of Hosts. Think of the torture and death of Jesus, whose gory execution is celebrated every day in every Christian church way more than his life-affirming resurrection. Think of the parts of the Koran that urge people to spread the Word at the point of a sword. Think of the horrors done to Muslims in Myanmar as we speak, committed in the name of that Paragon of Peace, the Buddha.

Blood and guts. Blood and guts.

(Are you insulted by my including your religion in the myths of the world? Do you take the stories told about your favorite deity as history? As fact? Then I'm sorry. I don't mean to step on anybody's toes. I ask you to simply lift your religion out of the way of this rollercoaster we're on, but please stay aboard for the ride.)

Blood and guts.

We've already skimmed over the Trojan War. Skimmed it the way swallows skim the pond at dusk for bugs. Paris. Helen. Agamemnon's murder of his own daughter for the sake of a lucky wind. The burning down of a beautiful city and the deaths of thousands.

And so on.

But according to the stories, the reason for all this, for all the above, the very *beginning* of a reason for the war that shook up the Ancient World—is a hoot.
And a curse.

It seems there was an evil Goddess of Discord called Eris kicking around in Greek Heaven. (We have our Satan; they had Eris). This character created trouble between the Deities—jealousies, vendettas. Not that the Deities needed any outside help to bicker and feud, thank you. It came natural to them and they were plenty good at it.
But the other Holy Ones didn't care for her company very much, no surprise, so she didn't get invited to an important wedding when everybody else had been.

Oof! That hurt. Apparently even evil Goddesses had feelings.

OK, she said. They were going to be like that? Then take this! She tossed an apple into the reception party from behind a tree. It was of solid gold and Eris had engraved on it:

FOR THE MOST BEAUTIFUL.

Oh, dear.

According to the tale, "naturally" all the Goddesses wanted it. It was important to these ladies who ran a big piece of the world, its waters and its forests and its hills, its households and its animals, its wisdom for god's sake, to be The Knock-out Honey of Knock-out Honeys!

Imagine the squabbling and the cat fights (again according to the tale). Until the "contest" came down to just three contestants:

Aphrodite, the Goddess of Love.

Hera, the wife (and sister!) of Zeus (The Commander In Chief), the Queen therefore of the Gods, and also the Goddess of women and childbirth.

Athena, born straight out of the head of Zeus (ouch!), Goddess of wisdom (not so wise in this case), and manual skills, and warfare.

(Is this beginning to stack up like a TV show? Certainly like the Miss America extravaganza? I think I said not much changes about people besides technology. I didn't say that? Well, I am now and you can quote me).

The Gods and Goddesses begged Zeus to judge the three. "Which of us, O *Capo di Tutti Capi,* is the fairest of them all?"

"Oh, no," said he. "No, no, no!" He had been around the block and back and knew how dangerous judging the dangerous can be. A judgement almost always means somebody loses. And some losers were sore losers. And some sore losers took revenge.

And Goddesses knew plenty about taking revenge.

Remember the vengeance of Persephone on Eristhichon? Of Artemis on the young and silly Actaeon?

And one of the contestants was his wife, don't forget. So that if he chose her he'd be accused of favoritism. And if he didn't, he'd be sleeping in the doghouse for a century or two.

They begged. They pleaded. They flattered. He was the Main Man, they said. Nobody in the Universe was smart enough (and brave enough) to do the job!

Nope.

And that was final.

You could only harangue the Head God for so long before your legs got broken or your teeth loosened.

But…maybe Zeus could help them out anyway. He happened to know that on a hill outside of the great city of Troy, a fine young man was sitting against a tree playing a flute to keep his herd of goats happy. This boy, Paris, was actually the son of the King of Troy.

A Prince, can you believe it, herding goats. Zeus knew that the reason the Prince of Troy was stuck in the boonies was because King Priam, his father, had heard a very disturbing prophecy. Paris, it said, would be the ruin of his magnificent city. So the King kept the kid outside the city limits.

But Zeus didn't bother telling his Gods and Goddesses all that. Why not? Don't ask me. As we all know by now, the ways of God (or Gods) are mysterious. Remember Jehovah's famous answer to Job? More or less, *Sit down and shut up, chump! You're in no position to ask Me to explain anything!*

Yes, *Sir!*

What Zeus did say is that Paris would make a good judge of feminine beauty, since despite his tender years he had sampled a surprisingly large chunk of it for himself.

Of course the contestants agreed with Zeus's "suggestion." One normally does not disagree very much with a Supreme Being.

Imagine the surprise of Paris when an entire wedding party of Deities dropped out of a cloud! I see him there, surrounded by sheep shit, frozen in mid-toot on the flute.

(If I were Paris I would have run like hell when I heard from the dazzling crowd what my job was supposed to be. Maybe this freaked-out kid *did* try to run. But you can't escape the will of the gods.
Uh-uh.
Don't they say when a horrible thing takes place, "It was God's will?" Excusing it somehow? And also letting you know there was not a damned thing you could have done about it?)

That poor kid, though. That Paris! He had had a good time with many women and girls. But this trio? They were the very *Ideals* of Beauty! They *blinded* with their beauty. Just looking at them was like staring into lit light bulbs.

But after the lad had stammered and twitched for a half-hour, unable to decide, or afraid to say, who was the most gorgeous of the three, the ladies offered to help.

By presenting bribes!

What?

Uh-huh. Their reasoning was, *Deciding between the most beautiful women in the Universe was obviously over the head of this redneck, no matter that Zeus swore by him. But maybe the kid could decide on the juiciest Birthday Present!*

Yes. That was more like it.

Hera promised Paris if he chose *her* to be the Beauty Queen, she'd make him Emperor of Europe and Asia. And she could do it. She was the wife of Zeus. She was the Queen of Greek Heaven. An Emperorship was a piece of cake for a Queen of Greek Heaven.

The kid's eyes crossed in excitement.

But then Athena stepped up before he could say a thing. If Paris chose her, she'd arrange to have him lead the Trojans in a victorious war against their archenemy, the Spartans. That would bring more honor and riches to him than he could think up. And girls. Here the eyes of Paris spun around like lights on a cop car. He loved girls. We know that. But he was also a scaredy-cat, famous for slinking away from brawls. So the idea of having macho medals pinned on him and a laurel crown perched on his head was just about enough to push Paris over the edge.

Until the Goddess of Love, Aphrodite, sashayed up and whispered in his ear, if he chose her he would have by his side and in his bed the most beautiful woman in the world, bar none. Even though the Goddess knew the woman who fit that bill was the famous Helen. And that she happened to be married to Menelaus, the King of Sparta.

(Whatever...)

Trouble! Right?

But Paris chose Aphrodite. Just like any other young fool thinking not with his brain but with an entirely different organ. He evidently didn't see that if he were made Emperor of everything, he could have money and power with no limits—*and* the Most Beautiful Woman in the World, if he wanted her too.

Duh.

He handed the Goddess of Love the golden apple.

Didn't I say the so-called Judgement of Paris was a hoot. But I also said it was a curse. Because that judgement, or choice, made by Paris destroyed a fabulous city, caused the death of thousands, and turned the Ancient World on its ear.

Here's our poet again, having something to say about the above:

HELEN

Believe me,
it wasn't only her face that launched a thousand ships.
Every inch of her swelled and melted
like moonlit surf.
Only where the ocean is frigid,
she was hot.
. . . .
Menaleus, you greybeard,
you were lucky enough to marry the maid,
and dumb enough to have young Paris over.
They didn't name the city for this boy for nothing.
In his young studly way
he was as golden as Helen.

Menelaus, dim husband,
were you blind to the tunnel
that opened between the liquid children?
Were you deaf to the sudden beat of hearts
becoming drums?

Then you couldn't have heard the wheels turning in Heaven
arranging the war that tore the ancient world,

that gave poets something to write about forever,
when the boy stole the girl.

But I also called the story a curse because that's what it makes me want to do.

I fucking hate that story! (See what I mean?) I hate it because like so many other Western myths, tales, stories, novels, movies, TV shows for the last two or 3,000 years, it dumps on women. It shrinks them down. It shoves them underneath men, politically and physically. And in this case, morally. The story off the Trojan War is bad enough, but it's the Judgement of Paris business that really pisses me off.

Here we have the very highest exemplars of women. Hera, the Female Supreme Being. Athena, supposedly the Goddess of Wisdom, for Chrissake! And Aphrodite, the Goddess of Love, and therefore the most important of them since, in my opinion anyway, love is the most sacred of impulses in the Universe. So the highest of women, don't you know, behaving like silly High School girls, to put it kindly. Less kindly, like the worst sort of corporate lobbyists in the US Capitol.

("Havin' a hard time makin' up yo' mand, Sen'tor? Well, do nann gazillion bucks hep you to? And you know on whut side to mark yo' X, rat? Still unsure? Well, would another gazillion clear thengs up?")

The highest of Goddesses in the Ancient Greek set-up have a cat-fight about shallow physical cutesiness. Making goo-goo eyes at a boy. While Zeus, the Alpha Male, the champ of rapists, laughs up his sleeve.

This is all harmless fun, right? It's all this old-timey stuff, right?

In other words, so what?

Here's what. Look around. There are three main religions in the Western World. Do you see a woman God sharing divine power with a male God in any of them? Even though there are as many (if not more) women around as men? Even though women are at least as intelligent (if not more) and capable as men? Even though the natural world, Nature, is basically female, as is the earth herself (giver and supporter of life)?

Well, what about the Virgin Mary? you say.

Yes. Blessings upon her! She's proof of how strong the instinct is for a feminine deity, the *need* for one. She survived all the schemes of men to keep the female out of the sacred picture, once the Roman Empire was put down.

The Romans had stolen the Greek religious set-up pretty much in one piece. And that meant a Father God, sure. But also a whole stack of powerful lady gods, including the Father God's wife.

Once the Roman gang was converted to Christianity though, all those wayward and sexy gods and goddesses were dumped (or promoted downstairs to sainthood) to make way for God the Disciplinarian and his Son. Not his daughter, notice. But Son.

Yet the Mother of that Son refused to fade away. She stands in every Catholic and Episcopal Church in the West, and if I'm not mistaken, in every Orthodox Church in the East. She apparently has some influence with God, just as Hera did with Zeus. And so millions pray to *her* for help, for favors, for forgiveness, and so on.

She knows somebody in City Hall, see.

She's a great mother. She doesn't scold, doesn't lay down the law, doesn't punish. Love seems to be what she does. And she is widely loved back.

But she still plays second fiddle to God the Father, at whose side remember, sits the Son, not the Wife out of whose body came the Son.

Second fiddle.

Well, you college graduates might say God is actually neither male nor Female. Or both. It's a problem with translation, you see.

100

The original language the Bible was written in used a neutral *it* when talking about God. We changed that to a *he*.

All right, I'll take your word for it. But even if you are on the money about this, we did change it to a *he*. Not a *she*.

And how many kids are taught that God is sexually neutral, or…well, even more graphically, a hermaphrodite?

What I'm saying is that the lone male God in the sky is what seems to dominate in the minds of millions upon millions, though for some there is a Son nearby.

And so the subjection of women for all these centuries can be justified in a handy-dandy manner: *God wills it!*

Only now are women making any headway in the Sea of Testosterone. But still they are fought every inch of the way by the Swingin' Dick Boys.

To show Hera, Athena, and Aphrodite as shallow bimbos certainly didn't help. That story, like so many others, added to the ripple effect that created the Lone Male God, and the popular belief that women are inferior to men. And more than *that,* were created to serve men. And more than that, were created to be *used* by men.

And so more than half the world's population, the female half, finds it very difficult, when possible at all, to contribute their smarts, skills, and guts to the struggle for human survival.

Stupid!

As always, look around. But don't bother looking at cultures where it's taken for granted that women are one step above sheep and goats. Look right here in The Land of the Free, the City On the Hill. We now have a President who boasted of being able to "grab 'em by the pussy" because of his fame and money, who before a world TV audience praised the body of the wife of the President of France, as if she were a thoroughbred horse in a French stable. Then there's the US Congressman who just this week stated that if women were allowed to nurse (God forbid!) in public, then he would be allowed to grab their breasts in public.

Now there's logic for you.

OK. Enough ranting. Sometimes I forget myself. I get angry and forget that my job is storytelling. The ranting depresses me. The storytelling makes me happy. So why don't I just stick to that?
I have a feeling you've asked the very same question.
I'm going to get back on track right now.

But with a twist.

The Trojan War. Remember? A thousand Spartan ships sailed to Troy to snatch back that cutey-pie Helen who ran there with the Trojan Prince, the cute flute player, Paris. After 10 years of blood and guts warfare, when many Spartan and Trojan heroes fought their way into the books, the Spartan soldiers took the city and burned it down, thus fulfilling the prophesy that Paris would cause the destruction of Troy.

Blood and guts! The clash of swords! The blast of trumpets! The screams of agony!

Binga! Banga! Booma!

Or if you prefer: Sock! Pow!

Then the Spartans returned home. Unless they were dead, or detained by gods with axes to grind.

Out of this war that historians say really happened, we get mythical heroes like Achilles, Hector, and Odysseus. But I claim there were other great heroes around this business that are barely mentioned, or if they are, only as supporting actors, or villains.

The women.

Remember that horrible scene on a cliff overlooking the sea, where Agamemnon, Commander In Chief of the Cretan army, cut his own daughter's throat to satisfy some god's bloodthirst? Because somebody had missed a sacrifice or taken a leak in the wrong place? Or, as some accounts have it, he, Agamemnon himself, killed a stag in a place sacred to Artemis?

(Recall what Artemis did to the silly Peeping Tom, Acteon? A smart person stepped very lightly around *that* Divinity).

Anyway, something had been done to piss off some god who in revenge made the winds blow away from Troy instead of toward it, and so the brothers Menelaus and Agamemnon had a thousand ships pulled up on the beach like dead whales.

Finally appealed to, that super fortune-teller, the Oracle of Delphi provided the only solution: the daughter of King Agamemnon had to be sacrificed to appease the gods.

Harsh? Yes. The ancient deities could certainly make cruel demands. Think of the Old Testament Jehovah instructing Abraham to sacrifice his son to prove his obedience(!). To Him. Though at the very last moment, there's a save, a reprieve delivered by an angel emissary. These reprieves, these last minute saves that occur throughout mythology I suspect were written in later by writers appalled by divine cold-heartedness. Can't prove it, but I sense it.

(And I'm haunted by this: one of the old Minoan religions made a hollow bull of brass. (Was Daedalus inspired by it)? They'd lock a human inside it, then build a fire beneath. When the poor bastard roasting inside screamed and moaned in agony, the priests announced to the crowd that what they were hearing was the voice of the sacred bull.

Cute, right?
What twisted genius thought that one up?)

—·—

I refuse to think Agamemnon took the word from the Oracle lightly. "Yeah, sure, whatever…"

He must have—or at least I want to think so—he must have gone though agony. (The girl was in part the issue of his loins!) But not for long. The soldiers and sailors on those thousand ships were growing damned sick and tired of hanging around and doing nothing more interesting than shooting craps and fist-fighting each other. There was talk of giving it all up and going home to the wife and kids.

Agamemnon had to move. He made his decision.

The adolescent girl was tricked into visiting her Dad. Then he murdered her.

Dear Ol' Dad.

But what about Mom? The Clytemnestra woman? For more than ten years she waited for Agamemnon to return from the Trojan War. Hating him for his crime. Hating him in the deepest chambers of her heart.

Understand, the lady had *witnessed* her daughter's throat being slashed. She had, of course, accompanied Iphegenia to her promised "wedding." Momma wouldn't allow her young daughter to travel without her. The world was too dangerous!

No, no. She was at her daughter's side constantly until she was delivered, fluffy wedding dress and all, into the muscular arms of Big Daddy Agamemnon, who had enticed the poor little creature and her mother to the bluff overlooking the stubborn sea. And the bait was the marriage of Iphigenia to the great and handsome hero Achilles.

A teen dream.

So Momma saw with her own eyes the flash of the knife, the blood, the eyes of her daughter fading to stones.

(Here too, one version of this gory tale is that at the last moment Agamemnon's knife was stopped by Artemis, and a lamb was sacrificed instead of a girl. I've already mentioned my feeling about these reprieves. On the other hand, if this version is accepted as Gospel, Clytemnestra witnessed her husband *ready and willing* to murder the girl, anyway.)

And what Momma witnessed burned like a brand into her heart.

So she waited for the return of her murdering husband, meanwhile picking up a boyfriend.
(Her rage gave her license to do that, right?).

(The boyfriend evidently had as much interest in getting his hands on the throne as he had in getting his hands on Queen Clytemnestra).

10 years.

10 years is a long time, but finally the King did return, bringing along some young thing he had sweet-talked away from her walled garden, her little dog, her cozy family. And a couple of their kids he had made with her. Twins, yet.
So this Agamemnon monster not only murdered his own daughter before her mother's eyes (or tried to), stayed away from home for ten years supposedly to get back his brother's wanton wife (also to gather up a bunch of the legendary riches of Troy, you betcha), but then showed up on his wife's doorstep with a new flame less than half her age, and two babies to go with her.

I call that nerve. Real nerve. Do you? I do. I call that nerve as outrageous and obnoxious as an infected molar.

Clytemnestra did everything a man like Agamemnon would expect his wife to do. She hugged him and kissed him. Hugged and kissed the New Girl and her babies. Ordered the servants to cook up Agamemnon's favorite meal and arrange for a hot bath. Knelt before him to undo his sandals. Helped him off with his tattered and filthy clothes. Lowered him into the warm bath.

Then slit his throat. Clytemnestra slit Agamemnon's throat, while the boyfriend stood by the door to keep it all strictly private.

A private murder, unlike the murder of Iphigenia, committed before the eyes of the entire fleet.

I have kept this account simple, though Clytemnestra has been called the most complex woman in Greek mythology. I have not mentioned that the lady was a *twin sister* of Helen of Troy, and thus a knockout honey herself. I have not gone into the boyfriend, Aigisthos, who had big and gory reasons himself for wanting to see Agamemnon dead. I have not bothered to describe the eventual revenge killing of Clytemnestra by her own two children as soon as they were old enough to stick knives into her.

I've kept it simple because the point here is to show the heroism of this woman, aside from anything else. In an ancient world where a mortal woman was by definition second class, where she was expected to obey and serve her husband in every way and without complaint or even an ugly look, where she was barely allowed to speak, for cripe's sake—this woman, Clytemnestra, walked right through all of that and did what her heart commanded.

She decided to punish her husband for the unspeakable crime he committed (or was completely willing to commit) against their precious daughter. She murdered the son-of-a-bitch.

In an age where she was expected not to speak outside the kitchen until spoken to—by a man, of course—she spoke, all right.

Oh, yes.

With her hands.

(In Shakespeare's *Julius Caesar,* in the act of stabbing to death his Emperor, Brutus cries out, "Speak hands, for me!")

Clytemnestra spoke too. In spades.

Heroically.

———•———

Now let's examine a second heroine, which will be, by the way, the last gasp of this messy meander.

At the end of the 10-year Trojan War, most of the Spartan victors happily sailed for home. Some stayed on for awhile to rape and steal, but in time they also split. Menelaus returned with his naughty wife Helen, and most accounts claim they lived happily ever after. (Why do I find that hard to believe?) Agamemnon also made it home in time, as we've just seen, with a new girlfriend and a horrible sin hanging over his head. We've also just seen what happened to him.

But a hero a hundred times more famous than they failed to get home right off the bat.

Odysseus.

Yes, indeed. Odysseus was a famous warrior against the walls of Troy, and in fact came up with the idea of building a huge horse, filling it with soldiers, and having the rest of the fleet pretend to set sail for home—actually to a point just out of sight of the Trojans. The Trojans would figure the Spartans had finally given up after 10 years, had taken off, but had left the big horse on the beach as a sign of respect for the stubborn Trojans. The Greeks banked on them dragging the thing inside the city gates and using it as the centerpiece of their victory bash.

Drag it in they did. And that night the Greek soldiers spilled out of the horsey, cut Trojan throats, and opened the gates for the rest of the Greek army.

That's how the Greeks finally knocked out the Trojans.

Sock! Pow!

Hail, Odysseus!

The problem was Odysseus had stepped on a god's toes at some point, the wrong god to step on. Guess which?

Hint: the smell of fish.

Posiedon!
Natch.

(The Greeks were great sailors and fishermen. Being for a large part island dwellers, they had to be. So they knew plenty about the sea. They knew enough to fear it.

Real sailors fear the sea. They've seen too much not to. They've seen what it can do, all of a sudden-like. They are conscious every minute of what rolls beneath them.

That didn't stop the Greeks from using the sea as a highway and great source of food. But as in all other things, they thought up a god to pray to and make sacrifices to, in order, they hoped, to get him to go easy already.

It didn't always work. Greek myth is filled with shipwrecks and drownings and delinquent winds and tides.

And the god who directed all this was…Himself. The fishy one. Posiedon!)

Here's what happened. On one island Odysseus sailed into for the night, the big shot was one-eyed Cyclops, a true monster, a giant who relished human flesh. But even he was no match for smartsy Odysseus, the inventor of the Trojan Horse. The monster trapped Odysseus and his men in a cave and ate a couple of them a day. Like chocolates. But Odysseus managed to get him drunk, and when the big dummy fell asleep, burned his single eye out with a blazing log.

In this way the Greeks managed to escape the Cyclops, but not the father of the Cyclops.

Who happened to be…Posiedon! Again!

You know, if you are a parent or are buddies with one, no matter how horrible the kid is, no matter how the kid's behavior inspires images of strangulation in everybody else's head, the parent still loves it to pieces and will kill to protect it.

So Posiedon had to get at Odysseus. He hit him with storms. He smothered him with calms. He tempted him with hot sea-girls. He tried to crush him on rocks. He did everything he could to keep out of reach the one thing Odysseus wanted most in the world: his home.

It seemed that every time Odysseus sailed anywhere close to Ithaca he'd be blown far off by a storm that jumped up from nowhere. And no matter where he did manage to beach his beat-up boat and crew, he'd get tangled up in something—or someone—so that he'd be stuck there for weeks or months.

It took Odysseus 10 years to reach his island home *after* the end of the 10-year Trojan War.

The word on the street was he was dead. After all, the other guys made it home. Those who survived the War, that is.

But a few Ithacans kept the faith. A few old servants who loved Odysseus for his kindness and his jokes and his generous retirement benefits. His son, Telemachus. And most of all, his lovely wife, Penelope.

Pen-el-opee.

What a beautiful name.

But poor woman. Not only did she grieve. Not only did she cry herself to sleep in a cold bed. Not only did she have to raise a boy alone through his most hormonal years. Not only did she carry the responsibilities of office (she was, after all, the Queen and the only royal in sight since her husband was absent and her son was still a kid).
But she was at the same time tormented by these guys.

These guys.

We mentioned these guys earlier when we examined the sacred Greek idea of *xenia,* how a household was obliged to welcome any stranger on their doorstep, and how the guest was equally obliged to treat the household with respect in all ways.

Instead, once they had convinced themselves Odysseus would never return, these guys moved into Penelope's house! They moved right in there and lay around all day and ate her food and drank her wine and farted and belched just like the low life trash they were.

We've all seen low lifers like these. They're the ones who hang out in bars all day and watch the game and bellow at each other and work or deal just enough so that they can hang out in the bar all day and yell at each other and at the game on TV. For years.

In the Pacific Islands they call them "waste-timers."

And to top it off, these guys got it into their heads that if one of them could *marry* the grieving widow, not only would he get his hands on a knockout body, but he'd inherit the whole damn Kingdom! And once Mr. Lucky achieved Paradise, he'd, of course, take care of all his buddies. And without a worry in the world, they'd be able to happily eat and drink themselves to death.

Great plan, except that that stuck-up Queen would have none of it.

Imagine. Here was a great hall, rough around the edges, with its stones and thick rugs and huge fireplace. But still, a snazzy place, obviously the digs of a powerful family.

There stood a long table, and seated (or sprawled) on benches around it were the town loafers, the guys who never married, raised a family, found a trade, went anywhere, challenged themselves. Never, as Hamlet said, took up arms against "...the slings and arrows of misfortune."

Waste-timers.

But they saw an opportunity. *That* they were able to do. A scam! A deal! A killer deal!

They figured the lion was gone forever. Made sense. Why would years go by without him getting back to his throne, trophy wife, hotshot home, and even a son? Why? Because he couldn't, that's why.

Because he was dead.
Must be.

So there they were, the guy with the oily hair and beard, who thought himself a ladykiller, stud, cocksman, player. He made up his eyes like a silent movie star.

Then there was a fat man, his chest pushed up into his chin, so that to look down at his plate was impossible. Lots of times he had no idea what he was about to stuff into his face until he stuffed it into his face and tasted it.

There was the one they called Ferret. Another, Porky. Because... guess why.

There was also a lush. This mess stayed drunk as a skunk, 24/7. And looked it. Smelled it.

You get the idea. You've probably seen bozos like this, maybe rubbed elbows with them. I know I have.

Maybe you've caught on to how they would drag you down to their level, and below it, if they only could, since they can only stand up straight when they're standing on somebody else.

As the months rolled by, the "visitors" got bolder. Poor Penelope had to brush dirty fingers off herself all day long. And when her young son bravely came to her defense, he got his ass kicked.

"All right," she said one morning, as she looked over the junk-yard her house had turned into. "I surrender. Anyway, we're running out of food and booze and going bankrupt. So I make this proposition. See this tapestry I'm weaving? When I finish it I'll choose one of you as my new husband."

The bums agreed. They saw that the thing was half done. They could wait the week or two it would take to finish it. Because then...payoff! For one of them, anyway. And who knew? The lucky one might grow tired of the angel and consider...sharing?

A mighty interesting poker game might be played in that situation.

But that situation never came up. The lady was much too loyal, too noble, too *clever* to fall into those low life hands.

At night she undid all the weaving she had done by day. That way she held off the unspeakable.

How could anybody fall for that? Well, you needed a snootfull of booze to fall for that, and those boys certainly, as they say, met that condition.

But why did Penelope resist? She must have been terribly lonely and up against a wall. As was her son. Of course the guests were swine and we can be sure that helped keep her on the straight and narrow.

But from all reports, the deepest reason she fended off the nogoodniks was that she was the wife of Odysseus. She was the wife of him whether he was present or not. She loved the guy, deeply and passionately. And when almost everyone else had given up on him, she knew in her heart (or hoped madly in her heart) he was alive! Someplace!

Someplace.

Through it all—20 years of it!—she held her head high. She kept herself under control. She acted nobly and heroically.

We saw what happened when Odysseus did return home. He killed every last one of the low life shits. Then embraced his wife, son, and his throne, and lived many happy years afterward.

But can you imagine how differently this tale would have ended if Odysseus had returned, sneaked into his mansion in disguise, and discovered Penelope in bed with one of the bums? A bum who now had his wife and his throne?

What would he have done?

Killed the whole stinking crew, of course. But would he have killed Penelope too? Would he have killed her for being a traitor? An adulteress? A slut?

Or would he have understood? Would he have taken into account his long, long absence and the pressures brought to bear on the poor, lone woman?

Would he have forgiven her?

Though it's always fun to speculate, in this case we needn't bother. The story ended happy and clean because of the heroism of Penelope, a heroism that had nothing to do with hacking and stabbing. But the heroism of constancy. Of true nobility. Of sticking to it, though to almost everybody else, "it" would have seemed absolutely hopeless.

The quiet heroism of Penelope may have been the noblest of all the heroics in ancient Greek myth. And one we can especially relate to because that's the kind of *heroism* most of us need in our lives. Few of us are sword-wielders.

Very little Sock! Pow! for us.

But all of us need courage just to live, though it may be as quiet as sunshine.

THE END

SOURCES

Bates, Ernest Sutherland, ed. *The Bible*. Simon and Schuster, 1976.

Bell, Robert E. *Women of Classical Mythology*. Oxford University Press, 1991.

Bullfinch,Thomas. *Mythology*. Avenel Books, 1936.

Campbell, Joseph. *The Hero with a Thousand Faces*. Princeton University Press, 1949.

Campbell, Joseph. *The Masks of God: Occidental Mythology*. Penguin Books, 1964.

Grant, Michael. *Myths of the Greeks and Romans*. Mentor, 1962.

Graves, Robert. *The Greek Myths, Vol 2*. Penguin Books, 1959.

Hamilton, Edith. *Mythology*. Little, Brown, and Co, 1940.

Johnston, Alan. *The Emergence of Greece*. E. P. Dutton & Co., 1976.

Kinder, Hermann and Werner Hilgemann. *The Anchor Atlas of World History, Vol 1*. Doubleday, 1974.

www.ingramcontent.com/pod-product-compliance
Lightning Source LLC
Chambersburg PA
CBHW020628250626
47154CB00004B/1719